Sharing a Cigar with Che

Sharing a Cigar with Che

Brian L. Kerr

Cover by
Tanya James

CANUSA BOOKS / CANUSA LLC

Brian Kerr/CANUSA LLC
Merida, Yucatan, Mexico

www.briankerrnovels.com

Publisher's Note: This is a work of fiction. Names, characters, places, and incidents are a product of the author's imagination. Locales and public names are sometimes used for atmospheric purposes. Any resemblance to actual people, living or dead, or to businesses, companies, events, institutions, or locales is completely coincidental.

Book design © 2013, BookDesignTemplates.com

Ordering Information: Special discounts are available on quantity purchases by corporations, associations, and others. For details, contact the publisher at the address above.

CANUSA LLC/Brian Kerr – First Edition

ISBN 978-1-5405834-8-2

Printed in the United States of America

There must be something about the fact that I sent my book to the publisher the morning we learned of the death of Fidel Castro. I don't know what that might be, but something...

Thank you, as always, to my talented baby sister Tanya James for the wonderful cover.

And thanks, once again to my wife for allowing me to sneak away without helping with the dishes, pretending I needed to write. As always, my friends, family and neighbors in Cuba have provided me the fodder for most of this book, and most especially, to our dear friend, Mateo, may he rest in peace, for being the inspiration for this fictional novel.

FOREWARD

At his present age of eighty-nine years, Mateo had grown into a caricature of his former self. He had always been a tall man, but now he looked like he'd been stretched on a torture device – his legs seemed too long and his neck exaggerated by the extra skin that had nowhere else to go, so it made itself into two flaps that looked almost transparent. He had long-since given up any sense of pride in his looks, so the white eye brows looked like two small bird's nests attached to his forehead. People spent a lot of money to have their Schnauzer dogs trimmed like Mateo. He had lost a tooth somewhere over the past few years, and didn't seem to be looking for it. One ear lobe hung down lower than the other, or maybe it was just because his shoulders tilted unevenly.

Today was potato day for the quota, so he pushed a wheelbarrow that must have been used in the construction of the church in the main square of Trinidad, some five hundred years earlier. The wooden sides of the cart were scored so deeply they looked like the two sides of the boards would soon meet in the middle. The handles seemed to have been polished to a shine, but it was just from the years of having the same hands holding them in the same position. Those hands had turned so hard from their labor he could have sanded furniture with his palms and fingers.

Charlie Chaplin would have been proud of the hitch in Mateo's step as he pushed the wheelbarrow along the bumpy cobble-stone street, keeping rhythm with the little grinding noise the solid rubber tire made as it scraped the side of the fork where the axle was attached with each revolution. Revolution of the wheel, that was. Mateo had survived the other revolution in Cuba, but didn't much like to talk about how he'd been forced from his coffee plantation up in the mountains of Topes de Collantes, just because he'd allowed the government soldiers to kill his remaining ten chickens. It wasn't like he'd had a choice in the matter. The revolutionary soldiers had killed his goats not more than a week earlier, and he'd given them shelter in his small barn.

Now, after nearly thirty-five years as chief quality inspector for the lucrative Cuban coffee industry, Mateo's full pension from the government translated to about six U.S. dollars a month. The small house he had been allotted in Trinidad when he'd moved back with his sisters and later his wife, needed repairs, and one sack of cement cost more than his monthly pension.

PART ONE

As though he didn't already work hard enough to keep in prime shape, Mateo had a secret passion for exercise, and had fashioned his own private gymnasium in the shade of the big tree behind the shed where he roasted coffee to sell to the hotels and restaurants in Trinidad. At over six feet in height, Mateo was a striking figure in the community. Heads turned when he walked past, his strength evident in his walk and the way his chest filled the grey work shirts that he usually wore. He would get the fire just right to toast the coffee for the week's orders, then begin his routine. The metal pipe that was left over from one of his plumbing jobs was just right for the chin-up bar, which he welded to a strong frame and bolted firmly above the open window outside the shed. It was more than ten feet from the ground, but Mateo could easily reach it with a strong hop from below. He would do dozens of chin-ups while he watched the process of the roasting through the window. When it was time to move the beans, he would hop down and use the t-shaped rake he'd welded to move them around and ensure they roasted evenly. Then he'd head back to his gym and lift the engine parts he'd attached to another pipe. He'd found two pieces at an old junk heap that weighed the same amount, and carried them home more than three kilometers. He wanted to be strong enough for anything he needed to do on the farm. And besides, he liked the way he looked with his bulging arms and barrel chest. His light brown hair was also a rarity. Most of the people he knew had typical Cuban features – black hair and dark brown eyes. Mateo's grandfather was Scandinavian, and had come to Cuba to be with his grandmother, whom he'd met while she was studying in Czechoslovakia. He favored his grandfather, while his sisters were darker, like their mother. Two of them were tall, too, and strikingly beautiful, while the youngest had suffered from fevers as an infant and it had stunted her growth. People teased her about being the ugly step-sister, and he'd made some of them very sorry to have made his sister cry.

Another strange thing about Mateo was his habit of counting out loud. He counted everything he did – when he pulled weeds from the garden, he counted them as he tossed them onto the pile between the rows. He counted the chickens that poked around for bugs and worms. He counted his chin-ups as he watched the coffee beans roast.

Once every two weeks, Mateo would load his wagon with carefully packed bags of coffee, and head down the mountain toward Trinidad. He harnessed two horses, and led a second pair behind, to switch them for the difficult return trip up hill. His sisters packed him a large basket of bread and cheese and ice water for the trips, and his mother made sure his clothes were washed and crisply ironed. He would kiss his mother on the cheek, ask for her blessing, and give instructions to his sisters to care for the animals, and to make sure no one snuck in at night to steal their beans. Four females and only one man. Mateo claimed that not even the dogs they cared for were males. He would make a joke of it when he saw the sad face of his wife. She always felt she had failed him.

On his way down the winding road toward Trinidad, he counted the telephone poles as he passed each one in turn, and sometimes he counted the revolutions of the wheels of the old cart between the telephone poles. There was a little piece of cloth stuck in a repair in one of the old bald tires, and that was his indicator to count the revolutions. People who knew him, and his strange custom began to call him "Counter", behind his back. Few had the nerve to find out if he would be angry if he knew they called him a name. People made little jokes, quietly, out of his earshot, calling him "Counter-intelligence" and "Counter-revolutionary". They stopped those little jokes when a government person, secret police, they assumed, came around asking questions about his activities.

Mateo hadn't appreciated that one bit, and spent the following few days doing his own investigation into why he'd had the visit. It was lucky for a few neighbors that everyone gave him the same answer… they had no idea. One look at the bulging muscles stressing the seams of his shirts was enough to give all of them amnesia at the same time.

The other prize possession of his father was a watch that he had been handed down by his grandfather, to his father, and then to him. It was the kind of watch that opened up to read the face, and had a big winder where the silver chain joined to the watch. It had an eagle etched into the silver on the front, and an engraving inside, that simply said, "For my son," with the date of March 13th, 1828 under it. One of his forefathers had given it to his son, and it had been passed to the first-born son in every family since then. Mateo would look on with reverence as his father wound it every night before he went to bed, just as his father had shown him, and his father before that. Other kids dreamed about bicycles and television sets, but Mateo just waited for the watch. His father wore it on his belt every day, flipping it open to check the time, so that he would come in from the fields for meals. At night, though, Mateo would sneak into his parents' room, crawl over to where the watch lay on the night stand, and quietly slip away to his room with it, where he would place it between his ear and the pillow, listening to the click, click, click. He counted the clicks until he reached sixty, then started over again. Time after time after time. The rhythm of the clicks became part of his very being, minute after minute that became hours and hours. He would take it away from his ear and continue to count, one minute (check the watch), five minutes (check the watch), until he could tell the hour and minute without any help from the watch at all. He would slip it back onto the nightstand before his father woke up, always stroking it tenderly. After months and years of this nighttime routine, Mateo would challenge himself out in the coffee plantation with his father. "Hey Dad, is it noon?" His father would flip open his watch and look at him with his eyes all squinty, as though wondering how much of a coincidence it could possibly be that it was precisely 12:00. Mateo would wink at him, and tell him that his stomach knew when it was time to eat. "Hey Dad, isn't it about 7:00 – time to feed the animals?" Crooked look, little wink.

His sisters were still very small, then, and already it was clear that the youngest had some sort of growth problem. She wasn't developing like his other two sisters. Something was out of sorts with her hips, it appeared, and while her upper body grew normally, her legs seemed to get wider, but not much longer. She was very late learning to walk, and seemed to be content to crawl around the house like a chimpanzee, but thanks to the encouragement of her sisters, and her mother's unfailing patience, little Corina eventually found a way to get up on her crooked legs and balance herself. Her physical shortcomings were made up for with her beautiful spirit and attitude. She wanted no extra help to do any of her activities, and did her best to keep up with her older sisters. Her idol, though, was her big brother, Mateo, whom she called Teo. He never tired of picking her up and tossing her in the air and letting her ride on his massive shoulders whenever there was someplace to go.

Mateo had always been a gentle giant, never playing rough with his cherished sisters. Since he didn't have a brother, or any male cousins, for that matter, he had no one to rough-house with. His father wasn't the playful type, either, so when the three boys made some hurtful comments about his baby sister that made her cry, he told his oldest sister, Lisbet, to take their other sister Heidi and Corina home.

The three boys laughed at his seriousness, and how he waited until his sisters were out of earshot before he challenged the boys to apologize for their actions with his baby sister. The fact that two of them carried baseball bats didn't seem to register at all with Mateo. He was defending the honor of his sister and his family, and he would take his lumps in the process. Mateo had never had time to play baseball, being the only son on a busy farm, so he was surprised at how brittle the first bat swung at him was. He had caught it in mid-swing with his left hand, using the trajectory and momentum to throw the batter to the ground several yards away. The bat in his hand blocked the next swing, and he saw the look on the other boy's face when he realized he was left with just the handle, while Mateo's bat was still intact. His look brightened, though, when Mateo snapped the bat in two with just his two hands, and tossed the pieces into the brush beside the trail. The kid on the ground grabbed for rocks to use as weapons, while the other two tried to rush him from opposite sides. He grabbed each of them by their belts and lifted them off of the ground, flailing like flies caught in a spider's web. He was trying to decide what to do with them when he felt the sting of a rock at the base of his neck. The pain shocked him – he'd never had much experience with pain, except for the odd kick from a calf during chores. With the other two boys still in his grasp, he turned to face the one who'd thrown the rock. He was preparing a second attack.

Mateo lifted the two boys until their faces were level with his own, and advised them to run home and get help. Something in the look in his eyes told both of them that it was good advice, and when they found their feet again after being thrown toward the third, they raced down the trail in the opposite direction from his sisters.

He knew the boy to be one of the Pomares clan, and this one was Ruben, he remembered from some coffee event they'd both taken part in a couple of years earlier.

"I hope you throw a strike with that one," Mateo said to his attacker, his voice calm and even. The boy cocked his arm for a hard throw, but thought he might have more luck with his legs, and threw the rock toward Mateo just so that he'd have a running start. Bad idea. Mateo's long, powerful legs caught him after just a few strides, and grabbed the other's wrist from behind him, locking it into his vice-grip.

The other boy flailed and twisted, trying to slip out of the grip, but Mateo held firm, and then twisted and turned until he made a pretzel out of the boy's arm. He then grabbed his shoulder with his free hand, turning him to face Mateo.

"Now, I think you want to apologize for making my sister cry."

"It's not my fault she's a freak," Pomares answered, spitting the words into Mateo's face.

"Wrong answer," Mateo replied, and released the grip from his right hand. Something snapped inside of him, and he felt hatred for the first time in his life. He lost control for the first time, too, and punched the boy in the face, crushing his nose and shattering most of the teeth in front in the process. He saw the blood spurt from the nose, and saw teeth fall from the boy's jaw, and his eyes went white in his head as he passed out, still hanging from Mateo's left hand.

He panicked, then, thinking he might have killed the boy, and swung him over his shoulder and ran in the direction of the other boys, calling for help as he went. He had to wipe the tears from his eyes to see where he was going.

That would be the last time Mateo would hit anyone in his life, if he could help it. He prayed the boy would survive as he ran to where he could see the two boys on their way back with one of their fathers. From his shoulder, he felt movement from the boy, and heard him crying as he approached the group. At least he wasn't dead, he thought, and handed him over to the other boy's father. He saw the terror in the eyes of the other two, and decided this wasn't the time for talking. He just turned and headed back toward his own home, finally taking the time to reach over his shoulder to rub the wound from the rock. He could feel the blood on his shirt, and knew his mother would be angry about the stain.

He wiped his own eyes as he walked, knowing he hadn't felt any better for having caused so much pain to the other boy. He knew he shouldn't have resorted to violence so quickly. He even thought about how he would have liked to have one of those bats intact, to play in the fields. He knew he was going to be in big trouble when he got home, but he figured he'd just as soon get back there and take his punishment. It was after four o'clock, he knew. Actually, he knew it was 4:13, exactly, and he had pens to clean before dinner.

Obviously, the three boys had a very different version of the events, and Ruben's parents had called the local police to press charges against the very violent and dangerous Mateo. His jaw required surgery and he would eat soup through a straw for a few weeks, until the wires holding it in place could be removed. In their version, Mateo had used the bat to break the boy's nose and jaw, and a bat was considered a dangerous weapon. Neither of the other boys had been anywhere near when he'd hit the third, but they'd agreed on the story, and it was three against one.

The police officer who visited his home the following morning happened to be a relative of one of the boys, and he insisted on immediate compensation for all of the damages and fees incurred. When Mateo's father asked for receipts to be provided for the expenses, he was met with an immediate threat of having Mateo transferred to a youth camp for violent offenders. A large spring calf and all of the cash they had in the house was the agreed-upon compensation, even though everyone knew it was three times the cost of the medical bills.

Mateo was distraught for days, hardly touching the food on his plate, and keeping to himself behind the coffee roasting shed when he wasn't doing chores or picking coffee. He knew his actions had cost his family a heavy price, and that calf would have provided necessary food and clothing for him and his sisters.

His father, a man of few words, finally caught up with him while Mateo counted his chin-ups out loud.

"I hope you're making that up, and you haven't actually done a hundred and fifty chin-ups," he stated, surprising Mateo, who had been facing the opposite way, watching the ovens through the window as he counted.

"I can do three hundred, some days." Mateo dropped to the ground, not wanting to make eye contact with his father. He still felt too much shame.

"I'm glad you're strong, Son. Your life is not going to be easy, with three sisters to look out for, and especially the way Corina is, you know." Mateo glanced up at his father, surprised he'd even mentioned her handicap, never ever speaking out loud about it. "I want you to know that I believe your story, one hundred percent. But I also need you to know that strength like yours needs to be controlled, always. You'll always be the villain, no matter what the situation."

"I asked him to apologize for what he'd said to Corina. I didn't want to hit him. But when he laughed and called her a freak again, I couldn't help myself." Mateo's eyes filled with tears again, feeling the anger return. "I'm so sorry for causing the family so much trouble, Dad. I want to repay you."

His father did a rare thing, then. He reached up and put his arm over his son's shoulder, pulling him close enough to kiss him on the top of the head. "Son, in the spring we'll have another calf, and we'll sell some more coffee to pay the bills. It'll be behind us soon enough. But that Pomares boy – he'll wear the scars of what he did for the rest of his life, and I doubt he'll call your sister, or anyone else, hurtful names after this. Your mother wouldn't want to hear this, but I'm proud of your for defending your sister, and I'm proud that you're so capable of defending yourself. Now, tell me what time it is, so we can go and eat."

Mateo allowed himself a smile, and thought about it for just a few seconds. "It's six-twenty-six. Do you want to know the seconds?"

His father flipped open his watch, and shook his head. They never spoke again about the incident.

"You know this watch has been passed down through many generations, don't you, Son?" his father flipped it open and shut as he walked with Mateo toward the house. "And you know it's never stopped, even once, in more than 150 years."

"I know, Dad, and I know how many times you need to wind it every night." Mateo looked at the watch like it was the most precious jewel anywhere.

"And you know that you're my first and only son, so this watch will be your responsibility when I'm gone, until you pass it to your first son, or your first child, if you don't have a son." Mateo couldn't imagine not having a son.

"I know, Dad. You know I'll take good care of it."

Whether his father knew more than he was saying, or if it was just a coincidence, within a month Mateo's father began to tire more than normal, and within a few weeks after that his skin color was very strange, almost grey. Mateo and his mother insisted that he see the doctor in Trinidad the next trip down the mountain with the coffee. Mateo joined him on the trip, and his father had trouble sitting upright on the sacks of beans. Mateo stopped where there was a wide space on the road and arranged the sacks so that his father could rest comfortably and he slept for most of the day. Mateo made sure he drank frequently from the bottles of cold water he had brought. He never imagined that his father wouldn't make the journey back up the mountain.

The doctor at the hospital was busy tending other patients, so Mateo helped his father to sit in the shade outside the emergency entrance, across from the canal that was empty most of the year, but filled to overflowing during the high rainy season. From where they sat, they could see two rats scampering from drain hole to drain hole. They were there for more than an hour, keeping watch on the wagon full of coffee. Mateo moved the horses twice to keep them in the shade. The hospital was in the center of the small colonial city, and it seemed as though everyone passed by at some time of their day on their way to or from whatever they were doing, legally or illegally, to make ends meet for the day. Everyone carried a dark bag over their shoulder, which would hide what they were buying or selling, and one or two plastic bags protruded from a pocket, ready to be filled with whatever fruit or vegetable was being sold from an open window or corner wheelbarrow. There were two main enemies in Cuba – the first was the supremely controlling government, full of inspectors and police determined to make every facet of every life impossible. The second was hunger, which trumped the fear of being caught by the inspectors. An avocado appeared in a window, and a ten peso bill that had been folded and unfolded so many times it felt more like a piece of old cloth, would slip between the protective bars and the avocado would get slipped into the plastic bag in one fluid motion.

People who saw the sacks of coffee began to ask who the owner was, to see if they could buy some cheap, to resell in their neighborhoods. Mateo knew he could make more money this way, but he would leave his father's regular customers angry. They preferred to make less money, but have more regular customers. The real danger was when he told people he couldn't sell them any, these were the same ones who were capable of throwing a sack over their shoulder when he wasn't watching, just to spite him. Luckily for Mateo, a cousin came by on his way home from the market, and he agreed to watch the wagon until Mateo came out from the doctor's checkup. He was sure his father just needed some vitamins that they lacked up in the mountain air.

The doctor was so black that it was difficult to see any expression on his face. Cuba had every combination of skin color, but after five hundred years, most were closer to mulato than either black or white. Mateo's pale white skin and blond hair were a rarity, and this doctor's deep black skin seemed to be pure African, with no mixture at all in the generations before him. He had a deep baritone voice that made Mateo think he was singing when he spoke. He came outside, to where they were sitting in the sliver of shade that remained on the concrete bench. He had his hand on the shoulder of the patient on her way out, and Mateo felt his genuine nature right from the start.

"What seems to be the problem, young fella?" the doctor asked Mateo, who had stood up when he saw the doctor approach the door.

"It's my dad, Doctor… he's been feeling very tired, lately."

"How long has he been this way?" The doctor was already hunched down, staring into Mateo's father's eyes.

"I first noticed it only about a week ago, when he wasn't up for morning chores."

The doctor's forehead seemed to fold itself into half a dozen wrinkles, and he pursed his lips, seeming to search his brain for something in his memory. It was just the way he looked at Mateo that changed the situation from routine to urgency. "Get a wheelchair out here, and take this man to my office immediately," he called to the orderly who was exhaling a cigarette through the half-opened door. The orderly took an additional drag on the cigarette, which was more than enough motivation for the large black doctor to rear up to his full height, and explode. "I mean NOW!" The orderly threw the cigarette to the drainage ditch and raced inside for the chair. Apparently, the giant doctor didn't raise his voice many times in a day, so when he did, people moved. It also made Mateo jump, and he looked to the doctor for an explanation. His father swung his arm weakly, trying to wave off the wheelchair. But he stumbled a bit when he stood up, and reached for Mateo's arm to steady himself. He tried to laugh, as though it was funny that he had lost his balance, but Mateo felt the weight of his father's body, holding onto him to keep his feet under him.

"Take him inside and get him a glass of water." Then, to Mateo, "Son, I'm afraid this is very serious. Mateo looked at him, his face forming a question and an exclamation mark at the same time. "I need to do some tests this afternoon, but it appears that your father has leukemia, and from the color of his skin and his loss of motor skills, I'm guessing it's in the final stages.

"What do we need to do for him? I have some money for medicine." Mateo reached for his back pocket, where he knew he had some pesos.

"Let's wait for the tests," the doctor replied, putting the hand on Mateo's shoulder that he had so recently removed from the lady who'd walked out. It felt comforting. He wasn't sure why his eyes had suddenly filled with tears. He saw his cousin wave from the top of the wagon as he followed the doctor into the hospital.

Mateo walked out of the hospital four hours later with his father's clothes and the silver watch in a bag. He saw his cousin asleep on the top of the wagon, in the same position his father had been half a day earlier, and it brought a chuckle to his face, for some unknown reason. All of his emotions suddenly turned to laughter, and he leaned against the tubular railing that led to where the two rats had become four. It started out small, then became waves of laughter that infected others around him. They laughed at his laughter, which woke his cousin on the wagon, and he laughed, too. The sun had gone down behind the western walls of the hospital, and the air was cooler. Mateo found his breath, finally, and stopped laughing, just as the doctor came out of the hospital and placed both hands on Mateo's shoulders. He told him the arrangements would be taken care of, and that he could come back for his father's body the following morning. The only thing Mateo could think to do was to walk over to the wagon and pull off a bag of roasted coffee beans and bring them back to the doctor. When the doctor saw the look on Mateo's face, he decided that refusing the gift was out of the question.

Mateo's cousin insisted on joining him while he made the deliveries of the rest of the load. By the conversation with each customer, it would have been impossible to know the pain Mateo was feeling. He carried each sack of coffee to every customer, just as though it was the same as any other monthly delivery, and the customer from whom he had taken the extra bag for the doctor assured him that it would be okay to make it up the next time he came to town.

At seventeen years of age, Mateo converted himself that day from the helpful son to the responsible man of the house, caring for his mother and three sisters. He used part of the money he'd collected to buy a new shirt and long pants and good shoes for his father, and brought them to the hospital, where the doctor had made arrangements with the funeral hall to bring a pine box to where they had prepared the body.

Fifteen minutes later, the nurses had helped to dress him, and the fresh horses had been harnessed for the trip back up the mountain. The casket was tied firmly into the wagon, and Mateo said his thank-you's to the doctor and staff of the hospital, and turned the wagon to the west, where he would eventually intersect with the street that curved onto the main highway between Trinidad and Cienfuegos, down the long descent that crossed over the river the fed into La Boca. A dozen kilometers down that highway, there was a fork in the road that led to Topes de Collantes, the community high up in the mountains where coffee and poor children are about the only things that grow easily on the slopes and cool, humid environment. Mateo couldn't help but confirm there were 190 telephone poles between the river and the right turn from the ocean view toward where his mother and sisters probably had received the news about his father. News had a way of covering the forty odd kilometers up to Topes de Collantes faster than any car or wagon, and bad news seemed to be doubly fast. Mateo was certain he wouldn't be the one to let his mother know for the first time that she was now a young widow, and to surprise his sisters with the fact that they no longer had a father. He had plenty of time to think about where he thought they should lay his father to rest. He knew it would be in the coffee bushes, where his father felt happiest. He remembered the tree they had thought about cutting down, because it was right in the middle of the trail they weaved down with the mules. His father hadn't cut it down because he said it was just too darned pretty to kill. Mateo was sure his mother would approve.

There was a squawking noise over his head as he ascended the first rise in the road up the mountain. It was the distinctive sound of the emerald green parrots that loved the climate in the mountains, and found plenty of fruit trees to keep them well fed. Aside from counting the seconds, minutes, fence posts, revolutions of the wheels of the wagon, Mateo had developed the ability to take a mental snapshot, like he did just that moment when the parrots flew over his head on their way to some other feeding area. Thirty seven parrots... several of them still young and not paired yet. In the snapshot he noted how many of them flew in close pairs. Something about travelling so slowly, in the open air, with the steady gate of the horses, made the wild animals less wary of him, and he noted the short little deer feeding in the brush off to the west, and the two muskrats, round-tailed cousins of the beaver, carrying twigs to their latest dam project. They ate as many of them as he could trap near their home – the meat was dark and rich, and best of all, free.

He wished he had a book to tell him the names of all of the different birds in Topes. There were hundreds of different ones, of all shapes and colors, from the tiny hummingbird that was hardly bigger than a bee to the eagles that soared high up in the cloud cover, searching for their daily meals. He made a point to ask the teacher at his sisters' school if she knew where he could find such a book. He knew in his heart, though, that after today, he'd have precious little time for reading anything.

He thought about how his father had told him they needed to buy more land and expand the coffee plantation if they wanted to improve their situation economically. He'd been grafting different plants together for the past few years, and it was clear they were producing significantly more and better beans. His father had wanted to grow the best beans in Cuba, and from the taste of the coffee they produced, he had been well on his way to achieving that goal. Now they just needed to produce more of it – a lot more.

It was July 26, 1958 – five years to the day after the famous attack on the Moncada Barracks in Santiago de Cuba. Mateo thought about the significance of that date, and how his father had always avoided the topic of politics and problems.

He always told Mateo his only problem was how to roast more coffee beans in a day, and just as long as they left him alone to tend his land, he didn't care who was in the big offices in Havana. He'd never been there and never hoped to go. Mateo had still been in school, then, in sixth grade – his last year. They'd had a visit to the school from one of Batista's local representatives, and he explained how bad it had been for people to raise arms against their own country, and what the word treason meant. He'd almost spit the names of Fidel Castro and his brother Raul. Mateo had chuckled at that, and got a stern look from Mrs. Aguila, who was a full head shorter than he was already. She had signed the papers allowing Mateo to leave school after that year, probably partly out of fear. One thing was for sure, his father could have used a good hunting rifle to keep food on the table, but everything that even resembled a weapon was confiscated shortly after that attack. His father had made an impressive bow, and wasted countless hours making arrows that never flew straight enough to even scare an animal, let alone kill one. They got their food from the traps Mateo set all around their land. He remembered how they had all laughed when his mother started strumming on the bow, telling his father that it was more useful as a musical instrument. His father had been angry at first, but when he finally started to laugh, he couldn't stop, and he even danced a little jig while his mother plucked on the bow.

Mateo laughed out loud at the memory. There hadn't been nearly enough laughter in their home over the past years, and there would probably be less over the next several more.

Parrots weren't the only things squawking up in the mountains as Mateo continued his steady upward climb, full of switchbacks and areas in need of repair. He would hop off of his perch to move rocks that had found their way into the wagon's path, for his sake, and that of whomever came along after him. One sharp rock could flatten a tire on the wagon easily, or worse cause one of the horse's to twist a hoof or even break a leg. Mateo needed his horses for work, not for meat.

Down in Trinidad, there had been news that Fidel Castro and Che Guevara were planning an all-out offensive, and there were troops from both sides converging in the mountains where the guerrilla-style forces of Castro were strongest. Mateo's father had been strong in maintaining himself completely disconnected from either side of the fight. If Fidel's troops wanted coffee or food, he would provide it to them. If Batista's men came looking for the same thing, they'd get the same. Just leave his farm the way they found it, and keep their eyes and hands off of the girls. Mateo's attitude had always been the same. They didn't own a television and the radio stopped working years earlier, so they had no horse in the race, as Mateo's grandfather always used to say.

As though it had been choreographed to Mateo's thoughts, he heard the distinctive sound of multiple vehicles gearing down to turn a tight corner, several kilometers up the mountain. They were big trucks, Mateo could tell. He scouted ahead for a wide spot to pull the wagon off the road until they passed. There was hardly room for two wagons to pass on most of the road up the mountain, let alone one of those big old six-wheel-drive units they used for hauling the lumber they cut up in the mountains. He found a spot to back the wagon off the road, with the protruding casket nudged between two pine trees. He un-hitched the two horses that had been pulling and changed their harnesses to the two that had been trotting behind. He hadn't planned on changing teams for another hour, but he decided to take advantage of the time he'd be waiting. He filled four pails with water from the nearby stream, and enjoyed the feeling of the water as he splashed it onto his neck and shoulders. He dipped his second-hand cowboy hat his father had won in a spirited game of dominos into the stream to let the fibers soak up a little moisture to keep his head cool once the sun found the back side of the mountain, which Mateo calculated would happen in less than two hours. He wanted to get as high up as he could before the hottest part of the day, and to have the horses in their paddock before dark. These trucks were fouling his plans.

Mateo found a spot from which he could keep an eye on his wagon and horses, and also spot the convoy of heavy vehicles when they rounded one of the switchbacks several miles up the ridge. He liked to calculate things, to keep his mind active, so he would figure out their velocity by counting how many seconds the trucks took to pass between two power poles that were visible from his vantage point. The first to show itself was a smaller Jeep with no markings on it. He could see four people in the vehicle, but they were still several kilometers away. He counted the seconds from one pole to the next, and began to calculate – there was almost exactly one hundred feet between the poles, so if they were travelling thirty miles per hour, it would take about three seconds to travel from pole to pole. He had counted five seconds, so that meant they were going closer to eighteen miles an hour. He knew they would be accelerating after the curve, but there were four more twists before they arrived to where he was. He figured they'd average about fifteen between straights and curves, so the Jeep would travel the five miles in twenty minutes. Just as he finished his calculations in his head, Mateo saw the front end of the first heavy truck. It was moving slower than the Jeep, but still moving well for a vehicle that size. It was indeed one of the six-wheel-drive logging trucks, with the fat tires and double smoke stacks belching black diesel smoke as it geared down to brake against the down-slope. The ones Mateo was used to seeing were always full of big pine logs to take down to the carpentry shops in Trinidad to be converted to furniture, or to the paper mill on the highway between Trinidad and Sancti Spiritus. Another one followed closely behind the first, and a third, slightly smaller, trailed by thirty seconds. When the Jeep had reemerged from behind the next switch-back, Mateo got a much clearer view, and saw that there was a gun attached to the rear. These were definitely rebel troops, and they were openly using federal roadways, which was strictly prohibited under Batista's watch. If they were intercepted by government forces or police, there'd be a battle. Mateo scanned what he could see of the road down to the highway where he'd come from several hours earlier, but could only see small slivers where the curves were exposed. Nothing heading this way that he could tell.

Nothing but him and his horses and wagon and his father's corpse.

The first big truck snorted around the next corner after the Jeep, and Mateo could see it had been modified to carry soldiers, and that it was full of them, now. There was nothing friendly about this excursion down the mountain. Somebody had plans for an attack, and probably didn't want anybody to know about it, including a coffee farmer on his way home to bury his father.

Mateo jumped to action. The first thing he did was throw the harnesses off of the team of horses, covering them with broken branches, and then led the four horses deeper into the trees, past the stream, to where they couldn't be seen easily from the road. It wasn't easy, since the terrain was steep, but he found a spot that was behind some large rocks. The wagon. It would be an obvious tip-off that someone was hiding there. He couldn't move it on his own, without the horses. And there was also that conspicuous pine box in the back of it.

He heard the rumble of the trucks on the last switch-back before they would arrive, leaving him fewer than ten minutes. Untying the casket, tears clouding his vision by then, Mateo tried to pull it out from the wagon, but there was too much friction between the box and the wooden floor. He knew what needed to be done, and how little time he had to do it. He startled two young deer that had become curious during the time he'd been stopped, and they bolted across the road and down the steep slope to the next group of trees that would camouflage them. Up on the wagon, Mateo shook his head, debating whether it was easier just to be caught there and take what came with it, but he'd heard stories of the treatment of army-aged men who hadn't joined one side of the battle or the other. They were enemies of both sides. Using the front of the wagon for purchase, Mateo bent his powerful legs until his boot heals wedged against the top of the casket, and pushed until he had no breath left. The casket had moved only a couple of feet, but it was enough that the center of the weight had shifted beyond the back of the wagon, and it tipped toward the rear. It continued to tip until the bottom came into contact with the ground, still between the two large trees. It was lucky that Mateo never went anywhere without the old machete under the seat of the wagon, because several branches impeded the trajectory of the pine box. He hacked at them expertly, using the machete's weight and balance to clear the path in only a dozen passes, and tossed it onto the wagon's bed to free both hands for the next phase of the project. Now that the casket had tipped itself to nearly forty-five degrees, Mateo knew it wouldn't take much effort to heave it up and push it over onto its top. He also knew what would be happening inside of the box while this process was taking place. A big acceleration from one of the diesel engines sounded like a dinosaur breaking wind, removing Mateo's benefit of time to think about the sound of his father's body slipping inside of the casket, while he pushed it past ninety degrees and sent his father face-first into the stream that trickled down the slope. No time to apologize or dwell on the situation. He swung the box to the side, and gathered the branches he'd just hacked off the trees, doing his best to make it look like a low bush. He ran to the road to see what it looked like from there, and it was reasonably covered. The wagon. The wagon.

The Jeep rounded the last bend before making a tight right turn, where there were twenty power poles before the curve where Mateo worked frantically. One of the young deer made the mistake of showing itself to the passengers of the Jeep, and the gun on the back of it swung around and took aim. There were a lot of mouths to feed in the trucks behind them, and even forty pounds of fresh deer meat would make for stronger soldiers.

Mateo had already spun the bolts off of the first wheel, but the third lug of the second seemed to be welded in place, rust and poor quality threads working against him. He moved onto the fourth, which squealed and shrieked with every turn of the big wrench. He dripped with sweat from the effort, blinded by the blond hair that fell over his eyes from the weight of the perspiration. Just that one to go. Mateo positioned the wrench on the rusted nut, and positioned himself on the railing of the wagon to jump down onto it.

The Jeep skidded to a halt so the young gunner could take closer aim. The little deer lifted its head to look back for its sister. That was its last mistake. The close proximity of the mountain slopes made an echo out of a simple hand clap. The sound of a high caliber rifle report sent a thousand birds of a dozen species out of the tree-tops like smoke from a back-firing exhaust pipe. The deer exploded from the impact, leaving precious little meat for the troops, and what there was would be hamburger.

Mateo was in mid-jump when he heard the shot, and sprawled onto the ground, sure he'd been the target. He checked himself for holes, and when he was sure he was intact, he looked back at the wheel. The wrench hung from the nut at a different angle, which meant his death-jump had been successful. He crawled on all fours back to the wheel and removed the last nut, pulled the wheel off and rolled it into the trees.

Just one thing left to do… Mateo crawled under the old wagon, almost wedging himself. He needed to call upon the last tidbits of strength he had, both physical and emotional, to finish this job. Grasping the short grass in his fingers, face down, he used his massive arms as jacks, and pushed himself onto all fours, the full weight of the wagon pressing down onto his broad shoulders and back. He heard the Jeep grind into gear, only a few hundred yards from the bend in the road that would leave him exposed. His father's smile entered his mind from somewhere, giving him one last burst of strength, and he pushed himself up to the full extent of his arms, and with his right leg as a lever, he clenched his teeth and pushed himself to an upright position, the wagon falling down the slope away from him, over and over. Without its wheels, the wagon was like a long rectangular tube, and once Mateo was able to start it going, it took on a life of its own, crashing and bending the tubular steel with each rotation into a more rounded shape. Mateo stood where he'd ended up, watching with awe at the spectacle he had just caused, hearing the steel call out in pain as it twisted and cracked like the cardboard boxes Mateo and his sisters played with when their parents had finished with them. He saw the deep gouge the corner made in the road as it bounced once before cascading over the edge and down the steep grade into the graveyard of vehicles that had underestimated the sharpness of the curve. There was a skeleton of a passenger bus at the bottom, and legends of the ghosts of the children who had perished that day back in the early forties.

It was only the sound of a voice barking an order to a driver that brought Mateo back to the present, and reminded him that he was completely exposed. He saw the front fender of the Jeep and dove into the long grass, where he would need to remain until the four vehicles had all passed by, only a few yards from where he lay. The grass wasn't nearly thick enough for his liking. He could see the road far too easily from where he was, so that meant if anyone was looking his way, they'd see him.

The bloody carcass of the little deer barely covered the hood of the Jeep, where someone had tied it as a trophy. Mateo thought of closing his eyes, like the story of the ostrich that hid its head in the sand to escape being seen. The Jeep was almost parallel to him when he smelled the cigar. A good cigar. He forced himself to look through the blades of crackling brush, and saw the image that would stay with him like a snapshot. Che Guevara, one foot resting on the back of the seat in front of him, a five day growth of beard, holding the cigar out to the side of the Jeep to let the air fan the flame, his head cocked back in a belly laugh, sitting next to Fidel Castro. Two buddies, out for a drive, without a care in the world, he thought to himself. The Jeep banged into the cavity in the road left by the wagon not fifteen seconds earlier, and Mateo watched as Fidel grabbed Che's shoulder just in time to keep him from bouncing out of the Jeep and onto the road. His cigar wasn't so lucky, and Mateo watched it roll into the dry grass fifty feet downhill from him. He heard the laughter, even louder this time, as they continued down the mountain.

Any second, the first of the troop trucks would come around the corner, and Mateo had another problem on his hands – fire! The cigar that rolled into the brush found enough dry material to ignite. It would cause the big truck to stop to put out the flames, and they'd find him there for sure. He didn't want to risk standing up, so he rolled over and over, wincing with every sharp stone he crushed against himself, until he rolled right over the burning area that was by that time a meter in diameter. He felt the blistering heat from the grass and stones as they seared into his flesh. He had no sooner extinguished the flames and covered the smoking grass with his body than he heard the behemoth round the bend, the sound of the big old diesel mixed with the voices of dozens of soldiers trying to talk above the noise.

He was exposed to three dozen trigger-happy soldiers, all hoping to try out their new toys. The only thing near him was the machete he'd salvaged from the wagon before it cartwheeled down "Dead-Man's Curve". All he could think to do at a second's notice was something he'd read about in the Independence War stories he'd read back in the times that he still had time to read. He reached for the machete, sliced his index finger along the sharp edge, and spattered blood on his face and neck, then wiped the blade again to cover as much of it as he could with blood. He positioned himself in what would appear to be an unlikely position for a living person, and made his best attempt at a death stare, mouth open, one leg bent over the other like he'd been thrown from the road. He closed his eyes until there was just a sliver of vision left, and watched the truck slow to almost a stop and forty pairs of eyes looked for any sign of life.

The internal clock in Mateo's head clicked the seconds in deafening cadence, like a thousand soldiers' footsteps hitting the ground beside his head. He saw the white tips of the wings of an eagle riding a stream of warm air, high overhead, and he wanted to smile, but dead men didn't smile. From the back row of the truck, he saw the face. In a uniform, with a long rifle in his hands, the creep he'd punched the previous year, looked almost like an adult. His nose was still out of place, though, and he'd never replaced the missing teeth, so the unattractive kid was now a hideously ugly soldier, and that soldier recognized him immediately.

It was all Mateo could do not to show the emotion that was coursing through his veins – the only person in the world he'd ever really hated. The only person he'd ever raised his fist to. Now that person stared down the barrel of his rifle as the big truck passed within feet of Mateo's blood-soaked neck.

"Now who needs to apologize, Freak!" the soldier screamed as he cocked the rifle to assure the person who had scarred him for life was dead. Mateo could thank the wagon for saving his life as the shot rang out just as the big right tire hit the crevice in the road, sending the rear left of the truck bouncing a foot in the air. The bullet hit the side of

Mateo's work boot, taking flesh and bone with it on its way into the rocks beyond. Everything in his being told Mateo to scream out in pain, and reach for the shattered foot like a cut finger reaches for a person's mouth. Survival instinct kept him still. He could scream and reach for it when the truck turned the bend in a few seconds. He saw the soldier cocking his rifle again, but they were already rounding the bend by the time he was ready for another shot.

The instant the truck and its cargo of hatred were out of sight, Mateo rolled himself back to the tree line and hop-stepped himself to behind the camouflaged casket before he ripped off what was left of his boot before the swollen foot became too large to get out of it. He saw how much blood was pouring out of the gap in his foot, and ripped the sleeve off his shirt to wrap around it and tied it tight, almost passing out from the pain when he pulled the knot snug.

The next two trucks lumbered past without anyone noticing him or the burned-out patch.

Mateo placed his head in his hands and rested his elbows on his knees. He stayed in that position for more than two minutes, gathering his thoughts and trying to make sense of what had happened. From somewhere deep inside, he didn't know where, came a laugh. It started as just a little chuckle, as the idea that he would tell Che Guevara, the revolutionary hero of all of Latin America -- he needed to be more careful with lit cigars. The thought of Mateo, the very image of a country kid, shaking his finger at Che, telling him he should quit smoking altogether, considering the problem he had with asthma, turned every emotion he had into laughter. He laughed for the pain. He laughed at how he must have looked, playing dead. He laughed at his father's lifeless body, twisting and bending and crashing face-first to the ground inside of the casket. Every morbid thing that crossed his mind came out as laughter. He thought about the neighbor lady who had a nervous problem that caused her to laugh in the most un-funny of circumstances. She'd be rolling on the ground if she was here with him, and he laughed at the thought of her laughing.

He didn't really know how long he sat there laughing, but his internal clock told him it was late afternoon, and he was miles away from any sort of shelter. It occurred to him to turn his father back to a more respectful position. He thought about using the machete to pry open the casket and fix his dad. On the other hand, he'd seen how his father slept in bed, and he was sure the position he was in at this moment was far closer to natural than any manner that he might arrange him. He adjusted the box so it was as level as possible, using stones and branches to prop it up. He had seen some color earlier when he'd moved the horses into the trees. He retraced his steps and found a patch of white and yellow flowers. He picked enough to make a simple arrangement that he could place on his father's casket. His first thoughts after the trucks left were to climb onto one of the horses and get home to his mother and the girls as quickly as possible. The thought of leaving his father alone, even for a few hours, though, knowing the strong religious beliefs his mother possessed, pushed that idea out of his head immediately. In Cuba, the family was expected to spend the first twenty-four hours after death with the body, keeping it company, and warding off any evil spirits that might want to interfere with the process of preparing for ascension to the better place above. Entire relationships changed based on who showed up at what time and for how long to a friend or family-member's wake.

Mateo didn't go in for all of that nonsense, but he didn't want to be responsible for his father's spirit not getting into heaven because he let his father's body remain without company during this all-important time. His mother would never forgive him. So he found a comfortable position, sitting on a fallen trunk of a tree, leaning with his back against the casket, and started a long conversation with his father, trying to keep himself from drifting off to sleep. There was so much he wanted to ask him. So much he wanted to tell him. He decided to start at the beginning, and tell him all of the things he remembered about his father. The list was long, and Mateo spoke out loud, and paused often, as though listening to his father's response. Most of the memories revolved around the plantation, the horses, the birth of Mateo's sisters, planting the coffee so carefully, spacing the plants just so. He recited all of the lessons his father had given him about when to pick the beans, how to separate the colors, how to prepare them for roasting, how to know when they were just right -- not too little and not too black – Mateo knew better than his father. It was one hundred chin-ups after the fire was the right temperature. As he spoke to his father, the smell of the beans roasting filled his head, the aroma making him wish he'd brought an extra thermos with him on this trip. His foot throbbed constantly, the pain horrific, but he used his conversation with his father to keep it from consuming his consciousness. He found another branch to prop his foot up above his heart, and that relieved some of the blood flow, making the throbbing less profound. Mateo even found himself chuckling out loud at some of the stories he recounted, including when he'd disobeyed his father and had climbed onto the back of the mule that was overloaded with beans, and it had bucked him and the beans off and headed into the hills. He'd spent two days picking up beans and re-bagging them. The next spring, they'd found some of the best coffee plants they had – the beans had found fertile ground and sprouted into what his father always called "Mateo's Folly".

He was surprised to see the sun was rising as he relived some of the events with his father. It was most unusual for Mateo to lose track of time. He stretched and scratched and willed himself to get onto his feet, or foot, as it were, since he couldn't put any weight at all on his injured one. His first job of the day was to hack a sturdy branch into a crutch, so that he could keep from planting his left foot. The cloth around it was saturated with blood, but it didn't seem to be seeping anymore. When he finally stood upright, he felt the dizziness of the loss of blood, and knew he needed to take it easy, or he'd pass out and might not wake up. He hobbled over to the stream, splashed water onto his face and drank as much as he could. Nature called, and an overturned tree supported him. He smiled as he thought of how the local newspaper would have been a welcome sight, always present in their outhouse in the backyard. This morning a handful of dried leaves was a poor substitute.

He cocked his head to the side, listening. There was a symphony of sounds in the early morning forest, but something was out of the ordinary. Something motorized. The sound was still too faint to be sure of anything, but Mateo tried to filter the birds, wind in the leaves, scurrying small animals, from the other sound that came and went with the breeze. He isolated it, finally. It was the sound of a tractor, laboring in its uphill struggle, probably too old to be working so hard. A tractor wouldn't have military people in it, though, so Mateo raced, such that he could, with the help of his crutch, to get to a place where he could make himself visible to the driver, once he could determine it was safe to do so.

He should have anticipated the tractor would belong to someone he knew. It belonged to the Sanchez family, who had logged in the mountains since before even Mateo's father was born. The driver was Salvador Sanchez, one of the four sons, and he was only a few years older than Mateo. He was alone in the tractor, and appeared to have a load of something on the wagon behind him, because the black smoke that rose from the exhaust was thicker than usual, meaning there was some weight behind him. Since the Sanchez family had a regular shipment of logs to the carpentry shops in Trinidad, the people who lived in Topes often contracted them to carry whatever they required from the city up the mountain. Sometimes it was a refrigerator, or auto parts, or even a dozen pigs. As he got closer, Mateo emerged from the tree line, waving to his friend. He'd forgotten how he must have looked, covered in blood and soot from the fire, his clothes torn to make bandages for his foot.

Salvador, or Chava, as Mateo knew him, swerved to avoid the crevice in the roadway, his face glued to Mateo, his jaw open. He stepped on the massive clutch that took all of his weight to engage, and popped the tractor out of gear in order to come to a complete stop, the load of heavy bricks and bags of cement behind him pushing him a dozen yards further than he'd wanted. The old tractor coughed three times before the engine shut down.

"Mateo!" he called as he hopped off the metal seat and ran over to his friend to take the weight from the branch. "What happened to you? Were you in an accident?" He was much smaller than Mateo, and struggled to find his footing with the extra weight, while at the same time trying to see where he was injured.

"I'll be okay. I ran into some trouble with a bunch of Castro's boys, on their way down the mountain." He stopped to catch his breath from the effort of hopping down the steep bank. "I could sure use your help getting home with my father."

Salvador looked around him, waiting to see his father come out of the trees. Mateo caught the question in his expression.

"You haven't heard yet, I guess. My dad died yesterday in Trinidad – he had a bad kind of cancer, and didn't last at all once he felt the symptoms."

"Good Lord, I'm sorry to hear that, Mateo. I saw your dad just a week ago and he seemed fine." The questioning look hadn't gone from his face.

"He's back in the trees, behind some branches." Mateo knew what Chava was looking for. It must have looked awfully strange, the whole situation. "I'm afraid I'm gonna need your help to get him home. I'm almost useless with this foot."

"We'll figure it out," Salvador responded, already working on the details.

He found a couple of big rocks to block the wheels of the wagon, and unhooked the tractor. He had enough rope to reach the casket from the road, if he backed the tractor as close to the edge as he dared. Mateo had hobbled back into the trees,

where he hauled out the harness and whistled for
the horses, who came trotting to him, thinking they
were about to get their daily feed of oats. With the
tractor, he decided it wasn't worth the effort of
harnessing the team of horses, and just placed the
heavy harness over the back of one of them, to get
it out of the trees. Chava tossed him the end of a
sturdy rope, which he tied firmly around the front
third of the casket, so that he could guide it through
the opening in the trees. The old tractor coughed
and sputtered; the clutch was a nightmare to
manipulate on the steep grade, but after three tries,
it found firm footing and inched forward in the
lowest gear while Mateo hopped along with the
casket, guiding it and leaning on it at the same time.
He smiled to himself, silently thanking his dad for
helping him, even after he was no longer alive.
Once they had the casket dragged up onto the road,
Mateo signaled for his friend to hook up the wagon
again, and pull it up alongside it, where he would
tip it up onto the back. They had to rearrange the
fifty bags of cement to make room for it, and
Salvador turned three shades of red by the time they
had finished. Mateo gasped from the pain every
time he put any weight on his left foot for balance,
and could see the burgundy stain on his homemade
bandage turn to crimson once again, with the fresh
supply of blood seeping to the surface. There was
a nurse who lived a couple of miles from his house
– she'd know what to do. He thought about his
mother and the girls struggling to feed the animals
in his absence, and felt guilty about that. The casket
was longer than the space on the wagon, and it was

Salvador who came up with the solution – he piled a dozen bags of cement on the half that was on the wagon, ensuring it wouldn't bounce off the back on the steep uphill climb to come. Mateo hopped around, tying two of the horses to the corners of the wagon. The other two would follow them by habit. Chava invited him to join him on the tractor, riding on the rusty metal fender, but Mateo had already fashioned a more comfortable resting place beside his father, on the remaining cement bags.

It must have looked like a strange train, winding its way up the mountain – a tractor, wagon, two horses attached, and two more following on their tails. Mateo had very little time to contemplate it, though, because a minute after they started up the slope, he was fast asleep, having completed the twenty-four hour vigil several hours earlier.

He awoke when his subconscious compass told his brain they were approaching his little piece of the world. He'd slept soundly for more than two hours, and had about two seconds of peaceful bliss before his brain reminded him of the situation at hand. Aside from being sick with worry about him, he knew his mother would have heard the news about his father by now, and would have had to break it to his younger sisters. He braced himself for the onslaught of grief when the reality of it set in of seeing the casket. Life was hard up in the mountains, and Mateo had already attended too many funerals of neighbors and family members. He'd seen the gamut of reactions, especially from the women – wives, mothers, sisters, daughters.

He wasn't prepared at all for the silence, the calm. No screaming, no wailing, no throwing themselves onto the casket as their neighbor's wife had done the year before when her husband had been killed by a kick from their mule. Mateo's father had helped to pull her off before they lowered the casket into the family's vault. It had been terrible. Everyone cried for her that day. So when his mother, Isabel, walked over to him, almost in a trance, he tried to understand her lack of reaction.

Silence. Deafening silence. Why was it so completely quiet? He saw his three sisters when he hopped down to the ground, and accepted the help from Chava to get him to the long wooden bench under the overhanging veranda. They were seated around the kitchen table, staring into the air. There were no lights on in the room, and the wooden shutters were still closed. His mother opened the shutters before any of the girls got out of bed every morning. Mateo searched for a reason why she hadn't opened them today. Grief, maybe... respect, maybe...

It was even stranger to him that Isabel hadn't reacted in shock and horror when she saw that he was covered in blood and had his foot wrapped in his torn clothing, and that his eyelids and lashes had been burnt off. The silence grabbed his attention again. No sounds. There were never no sounds on a farm. Animals didn't grieve. They grunted and clucked and barked and baaed and mooed.

"Where are all of the animals?" Mateo finally asked, finally turning to face the pens down the trail from the house.

"Gone, all of them…" his mother stated, matter-of-factly, never changing her expression. "Every goat, every cow, horse, chicken, even the dogs… to help feed the 'glorious revolution'." She emphasized the last two words, using the tone of the soldier who had said it to them.

Mateo closed his eyes against the anger he felt – hatred once again pushing itself into his gentle soul. His glance turned toward the coffee roasting shed, where there were still fifty sacks of beans, ready to be roasted for next week's order. His mother's skyward glance answered his silent question. "Coffee will keep the troops alert for the 'glorious revolution'," she recited again, still in her monotone voice.

Chava had removed the bags of cement from atop the casket, and had been able to lower it to the ground on his own, maneuvering it onto Mateo's front yard. He untied the two lead horses, and led them into the feeding area, where he found the oats and pumped water from the well for them. He dragged the heavy harnesses and hung them inside the barn. All the while he was anxious to get home to see what the conditions there were.

Mateo had been so busy wondering why his mother hadn't reacted to his father's casket and his injuries that he hadn't noticed she moved with a slight limp. That was new. It was when his youngest sister, Corina, broke into a half-whimper, that his eyes began to adjust to the lack of light inside the house, and he could clearly see bruises on Corina' and Lisbet's faces. Now the reason for the silence hit Mateo like the mule kick that had killed his neighbor.

Salvador walked over to where Mateo sat on the bench, but when he saw the way he was hunched over, his head in his hands, his massive shoulders heaving from the convulsions of his overwhelming grief, he decided it was best just to get home, himself. He gave Mateo's mother a silent kiss on the cheek, and felt her wince at the contact. He said a silent prayer of thanks he didn't have any sisters, but his oldest brother had a young wife. He waited until he was out of their sight, and then ran toward the tractor. He was still four miles from home, and wanted to waste no time in getting there. The tractor lurched forward and almost stalled out. Salvador had it in the highest gear he could, given the terrain.

As he willed himself to come back to his senses, Mateo tried to push the blind hatred into a corner of his mind. First he needed to take care of his sisters and mother, then his father, then himself, then… then… he didn't want to think about then right now.

"Mateo, it was horrible," his mother finally said, collapsing into his arms, sobbing from deep inside, sounds Mateo had never heard come from his mother before. She was living the perfect storm of all of a woman's worst nightmares rolled into one. She told Mateo how she'd barely learned about her husband dying from her neighbor who had a public telephone and had overheard a conversation she shouldn't have been listening to, when her daughter ran in to tell her that there were men tying up the goats and pigs and catching the chickens. She had no weapon, but had grabbed the pitch fork from the shed, Lisbet with a garden hoe at her side. There had been dozens of men, some with guns, taking everything they could see. Some loaded the sacks of coffee onto a big old truck, while others butchered the young calves right in front of her. The big stallion almost got the better of one of them, rearing up and kicking at him, so they just shot him and left him bleeding to death. When they saw the two women coming after them with their useless weapons, they realized there were no men to defend them, and the ugly one with the broken teeth grabbed the two of them and pushed them into the small shed where the oats were kept. He had another soldier lock the door from the outside.

Isabel stopped the story there, knowing Mateo needed no more details. When he could move again, he nodded toward the house, referring to Heidi and Corina. His mother looked off toward the mountain top, not wanting to face her son.

"She's just a baby, Mateo… how could…" Her voice trailed off, words not possible anymore.

As if to confirm what he already knew, Mateo felt a need to hold Corina in his arms and comfort her, more than the rest. He stopped mid-hop when he saw the word "Freak" scratched into the kitchen table with a big blade. He knew it had all happened while he was still in Trinidad at the hospital, but he was painfully aware of how many hours his mother and sister had been alone in their horror afterwards. He saw that Heidi had received the worst beating, her eyes both blackened and her nose still covered in dried blood. Still, she did her best to comfort Corina, who seemed to be fixated on the word written on the table in front of her.

Mateo knew this was far beyond his level of understanding. He needed help if he was ever going to make his family whole again. Knowing he couldn't walk the two miles to the nurse's house, he decided to make use of one of the few animals left, and hobbled to the corrals and climbed onto the nearest horse. The relief of taking the weight off of his foot was incredible. Given it wasn't a saddle horse, Mateo had to coax it to leave the corral with a few gentle kicks with his right foot, and he'd only taken the time to string a rope through its halter, so there was no bit in its mouth to help him to control the animal. Still, somehow it seemed to understand the urgency, and he only gave his sisters a quick, helpless look. This was a hurt their big brother couldn't make go away with a hug and a kiss.

PART TWO

After half a dozen trips down the mountain, Mateo had salvaged all he could from the old wagon, enough to fashion one half its size with the axle and wheels he'd stashed in the woods that day, nearly a year earlier, when the life he'd known had stopped so abruptly. The scar on the road had been filled with stones and rain and time, but the ones up the hill were still fresh. In the silence when he was away from the farm, without any animal noises to mask them, Mateo heard frequent gun-fire from below. He knew the revolutionary forces were gaining ground on Batista's ill-equipped and poorly-trained troops. Che and Fidel had proven themselves equally brilliant at guerilla war-fare tactics and propaganda, having taken control of the radio waves early on. Promises of dispatching the greedy American land-owners and eradicating the mafia-run casinos had struck a chord with the slave-like Cuban workers. Praise for a new democracy, hospitals and schools that would be built for everyone's benefit had swayed public opinion away from the puppet Batista.

Meanwhile, Mateo nursed his coffee plants back from the near-destruction of a year earlier, and sold horses to buy hogs and chickens and traded part of their property for two cows. He was out of bed and tending his animals and coffee plants long before the sun crawled over the mountain peaks to the east, and he seldom returned to the house before fatigue overtook him. The truth was, he couldn't bear to watch his sister Lisbet, still a baby herself at fifteen, care for the bastard son that had come as a result of the rape she'd suffered that day. He'd watched it grow inside her, innocent though it was, and dreaded the day he would share his home with the child of the man he planned to kill in the worst way possible. His father's name had been Mateo, like him, although he'd been known to all as Juan, after the famous Juan Valdez of Colombian coffee fame. When Lisbet asked if she could name her son Mateo, in honor of her father whose death had coincided with "the day" as they'd come to refer to it, he steadfastly refused. Mateo would be reserved for his own son one day, and the name would not be destroyed with the filth. She called him Juan as a concession, and Mateo choked down his acceptance. The child would have everything it needed, he'd promised, but it wouldn't have his love. Two months old, now, the baby was strong and healthy, much to his distain. The only good thing, he admitted, was the distraction it caused for his mother and Heidi and Corina. It gave them something to focus on besides "the day".

Not a day went by that Mateo didn't spend at least a few minutes tending the weeds and cleaning the simple headstone he'd chiseled himself in the shade of the big tree overlooking the coffee plantation. He smiled as he reminded his father he still knew what time it was, and how he had never forgotten to wind the old watch. He took comfort in the fact his father hadn't lived to witness the events that unfolded. It would have killed him many times over.

Ruben Pomares. Mateo saw his name on the headstone he planned to make for him one day. He cringed when he heard his praises sung on the radio from time to time, as he rose up the ranks in Fidel's army. To hear him mentioned along-side Camilo Cienfuegos and Raul and others was salt in the wound in Mateo's heart. He tried to avoid even looking at his sister's son – he didn't like to refer to him as his nephew – but the eyes were the same, there was no denying the lineage. All of the Pomares' had the narrow Chinese features, like they were squinting all the time.

Life in Cuba during the battle between the revolutionary forces and the government troops took on a new dimension that was previously unknown to most – mistrust and secrecy. It was hard to know which side people were on, and most seemed to want to know where their neighbors' loyalties rested. Mateo's rested solely on the side of his coffee plants and the animals and garden that fed his mother and sisters. He had almost no contact with anyone besides the customers he could still service in Trinidad, and when he heard a conversation turn to the subject of the battles, he changed it abruptly to the weather. His sense of humor had been all but eradicated on "the day", but for some reason, he felt comfortable enough around one of their long-time clients who ran a private hotel and served only coffee from Mateo's crop. It was innocent enough – Mr. Aguila had offered him a cigar, not knowing Mateo had never smoked. It had triggered an image, the way he had puffed on it and had such a satisfied look on his face as he held it toward Mateo.

"I don't smoke, but I once shared a cigar with Che Guevara," Mateo had stated absently, glancing up toward the green slopes of Topes de Collantes.

Less than a week later, he received an official visit from a serious-looking police sergeant, asking him questions about his relationship with Che and the revolutionary movement. The officer didn't laugh at all at the explanation Mateo gave for the comment about sharing a cigar with an enemy of the nation. He had received no official reports of the incident at the farm, or of the movement of Fidel and the revolutionary forces that day, which was an obligation of the citizen who had seen them. Mateo was asked to accompany the sergeant to Trinidad, where other military officials would want to hear his story. On the way down the mountain, Mateo showed him the damaged section of the road, the skeleton of his old wagon, and the spot where the grass had been burned by Che's cigar, still slightly different in color and growth from the area adjacent.

Having lost everything to the revolutionary soldiers a year earlier wasn't enough for Mateo, who received a heavy fine from the government for having withheld information and, most ironically, feeding the enemy soldiers. Mateo had no intention of describing the other atrocities his mother and sisters had lived that day, or he was sure they'd have doubled the fine for entertaining the enemy as well. How much more would they have added had they discovered there was another generation of one of the elite combatants growing up in his house?

Mateo left the following morning, not having slept, to find his own way back up to his farm. He was officially a man with no allies – a mortal enemy of the revolutionary forces, and a suspected collaborator with the enemy according to the government and military. And all he ever wanted to do was grow the best coffee in Cuba.

PART THREE

It was another New Year's Eve like the ones before it for Mateo and his mother and sisters, except for the fact there was an extra mouth at the table, and little Juan seemed to have an insatiable appetite. He was a toddler and found everything that wasn't on an upper shelf. Christmas wasn't any big deal for the mountain folk – that celebration was more for the wealthy in Havana, but Heidi had found a tiny wooden bat and a ball at one of the local kiosks and wrapped it in paper for the little guy to tear open. Something didn't sit right with Mateo, seeing the little version of his worst enemy with the same weapon in his hand that his father had come at him with, starting the whole downward spiral that was his life.

It was the closest neighbor who came past to wish them a happy new year who had heard the news about Fidel's triumph on his old radio. Osvaldo, the neighbor, had kept a steady vigil with his radio, and like a lot of his fellow poor and uneducated, took what he heard on the airwaves as gospel. He was preparing to celebrate the country's good fortune, and looked for the same enthusiasm from Mateo.

With his head down, his elbows on his knees, Mateo lifted his gaze to little Juan, who was happily beating on a chair with his new favorite toy. Surely next year, one of his sisters would find him a nice plastic gun. His permanent limp from the missing toe on his left foot reminded him of the revolutionary soldiers every single day. It was all politics to him, and it didn't much matter who won or lost – people drank coffee every day if they were on Batista's side or Fidel's, so as long as they stayed out of his way, he'd stay out of theirs.

Unfortunately, Mateo was the only one who lived up to that pledge. Fidel's thundering speeches from Havana had a new meaning every day. As though they were on a slippery slope with no grip on the tires, there was a constant turn to the left with each new day that passed. Things would be wonderful and blissful now that the evil Americans weren't controlling the economy. Nationalization of the country's resources was the key to Cuba's new future. Universal education and healthcare for every man, woman and child. There were subtle references to the glorious life in the Soviet Union at first, then not-so-subtle, and finally the Cuban population was hit over the head with it – the revolution they had fought so hard for was socialism, and Russia would be their big brother to guide them to its glory. Radio programs dispelled the rumors of hunger and long lines for essential products and services – all propaganda by a jealous American imperialist government, bent on world domination. The chasm of ideals that began to fester between Camilo and Fidel and others in the inner circle was down-played. Right-minded people were moved into positions of power and authority, and the train of socialist utopia pulled into the station in Havana. The people cheered and cried aloud at Fidel's enchanting speeches, and revolutionary heroes were paraded for all to see and adore. Fallen heroes were martyred and poems and songs were written about them to be memorized in the new schools, each with a bust of the hero of the previous war of independence, Jose Marti. Slogans were the order of the day, and the word revolution was touted as the symbol of everything bad about the previous regime, and everything that was good and fair and just and positive about the future. After gaining their victory with violence, Fidel began a campaign to disarm the country completely, because violence was to be a thing of the past.

Russia, waiting quietly in the wings, had ships already loaded with tractors and trucks and machinery and equipment to send to their little outpost only ninety miles from their arch enemy. The cons of giving up its identity to the Communist superpower were erased by the economic benefits of opening a tap of subsidies and support for the military that would keep the Americans nervous and prevent them from interfering in the new order.

Mateo didn't listen to the radio. He had no time, for one, and was too intelligent to be hypnotized into the bliss of the revolution as most of the population was. There was already discussion of where the new school would be built, and how many doctors would be assigned to the community clinic they had been promised. The revolution had already cost him a toe – he wondered how much more he would lose before things got back to normal.

Someone in the community had seen their local revolutionary hero, Sergeant Ruben Pomares, chest puffed out, uniform crisp and dripping with fresh medals, standing at attention behind Fidel and Raul during one of the televised speeches. The entire community buzzed with the excitement of one of their own at the top of the food chain in the new Cuba. Someone had heard he would be returning to Sancti Spiritus as the number one man in charge. Things would surely get better for all of them soon. Plans were made for a celebration when he came home. People used part of their meager savings to buy paint to brighten their houses and fences. The nurse who had helped Mateo with his sisters was seen around the village with a crisp new uniform, and had even dyed her hair and painted her nails. Apparently, Pomares' new fame and fortune erased his actions in her mind.

Mateo had his own plans for a welcome home party. This time, though, he wouldn't be foolish enough to tell anyone about them. Not his mother, his sisters, or even the cow he milked morning and night to provide milk for the devil's offspring growing daily in the house. He wouldn't love the boy, but he couldn't hate him, either. Mateo knew the child was innocent. Worse, still, Juan seemed to be obsessed with his uncle, and followed him around the house like a tiny shadow. He was beginning to form words, now, and everyone had heard him call Mateo Dad not long before. Perfect, Mateo had muttered in response to the girls' euphoria.

The small community was transformed by their collective belief they would be the recipients of special treatment under the leadership of one of their own sons. The verbiage of the revolutionary propaganda began to seep into everyday conversation – friends referred to each other as companions and partners, in keeping with the "everyone is equal" references in Fidel's speeches, which were rebroadcast endlessly on the radio until people could recite entire passages from memory. The theme of sending the wealthy Americans packing was a source of infinite pride. There were already plans to convert the luxurious homes of the business owners into schools and government offices. The Russian-style quota book had been presented in Havana, and crowds of supporters had screamed their approval – clothes, shoes, food, basic necessities – all were included in the magical booklet, and every man, woman and child would have one. Enough milk for every child until they were seven years old. The Russians had perfected the dream of socialism. No more rich people taking ten times their share. No more rich people, period. Filthy imperialists.

Mateo couldn't hide his feelings as much as he wanted to, though. When someone called him "Companion" on the street, he curtly reminded them his name was still Mateo. When his house was the only one along the main road through the community that hadn't been touched by a brush, people took notice. It was too small of a village for the people not to "remember" how Mateo had so brutally attacked and disfigured the smaller Ruben who had tried to reason with him. They talked behind his back about how the small fine they had paid was far less than it should have been for such a serious offense. History books and memories had been changed to suit the story that worked best. There were teams of historians busy writing the revolutionary doctrine that would justify every action of Fidel's band of merry men, as they had been called in the beginning, in reference to their Robin Hood-like method and philosophy of taking Cuba back from the rich and heartless to distribute everything equally among the poor and classless multitudes.

Only a few months had passed since the 'triumph of the revolution', as it was called at every opportunity. The word coup had been erased from the Cuban vocabulary, and dictatorship immediately corrected to socialist state. The wealthy elite Fidel had shouted about, fist pumping in the air in exclamation, were leaving the island to continue their evil ways in the land of the enemy. Their land and holdings were being redistributed justly for the common good. The definition of who was a wealthy imperialist pig, filling his belly at the expense of the true working class Cuba, began to change little by little in the never-ending speeches, and Fidel seemed to make up the rules as he went. A few words inserted into a phrase, especially when they were shouted with such passion and love for his country and the revolution they were all now a part of, caused a flurry of questions and pleas for explanation at the following round table meeting. In one of these, the wealthy imperialist pigs seemed to include any landowners at all, and not just the owners of the hacienda-style corporate farms who used slave labor and inhumane ethics to enrich themselves. Fidel was a landowner himself, after all, and so was Che, and Camilo Cienfuegos, and most of the rest of the revolutionary leaders. Definitions and clarifications and fine print were now being fabricated to point fingers away from the revolutionary heroes and toward anyone who either had shown sympathy to the Batista regime, or even indifference.

PART FOUR

The morning of the royal visit came and Mateo was up long before the sun, as usual. He had fed the few animals that remained, milked the only cow and strapped the harness onto his best mule in order to be picking coffee beans by the time the light crawled over the eastern peak of the mountain. He knew the city would be on full alert for the parades and celebrations that had been planned for the arrival of several of the country's new leaders, Pomares included. Coffee was the only constant in Cuban life. No morning began without a shot of the strong, sweet espresso, and no visit was complete without "toasting" with the best little cups a family had. All of the best would be dusted off for the celebrations, and Mateo had roasted and ground everything left in his storage area for the occasion. While the rest of the village would be on Pomares alert, he would be in Trinidad delivering coffee to all of his loyal customers and restaurants. He would take no chances – his mother and three sisters and little Juan would join him. He'd seen their frayed nerves at the mere mention of the son of a bitch coming back to town.

The wagon was loaded and in the barn from the night before, so they could hitch the horses and leave as soon as he returned with the fresh load of beans. He'd arranged with a neighbor's teenaged son, Alejandro, to stay at their house for the night. He would keep an eye on the animals and milk the cow that night and the following morning. The free milk was plenty of incentive.

As though the new facades of the homes along the main road wasn't enough, a thick fog painted the entire valley white for the arrival of the prodigal son. Mateo's mule knew the route by heart, its hooves falling into the same footfalls each time. There were forty thousand coffee plants in the colony. Mateo had been a mere toddler when his father had planted them, one by one, with a precision he had learned from his Colombian teacher. He had scouted the previous week, and knew of an area where the beans were prematurely ripe, the deep red beans hanging in bunches that made the collection fast and easy, not having to pick between the green and red. A normal man could pick ten large pails of coffee in a day, what a good mule could pack to the drying area. Mateo had his own system, and this day he would collect eight pails in three hours, so he would have time to spread them in the drying area before he prepared the wagon to have his family in Trinidad long before Pomares and his entourage arrived in their fancy Jeeps and uniforms.

The water from the well came out almost ice cold, but Mateo wasn't about to wait for one of his sisters to heat it on the single hot plate. He splashed it and rubbed the hard bar of soap against his muscular stomach to force a small amount of lather out of it, and cringed when he pulled the dull blade across his thick stubble. He only shaved when he was going to Trinidad to sell coffee, so it was an excruciating process, especially with the cold water. His mother and sisters were ready and waiting for him, so he hurried to hitch the stallion to the wagon. The load was heavier than usual, already, without the additional four bodies, so only the strongest horse was powerful enough to hold the weight of the load against the steeper downhill slopes. Mateo would use the wagon's friction brakes as well, but it would be a test of his still-weak left foot to hold the pedal against the wheel. He reached for his best cowboy hat to shade his face and neck from the sun, and a particularly strong breeze caused the beer bottle wind chime he had made for his parents to tinkle. Mateo had spent hours fixing the twine to the holes in the bottle caps and then used a pair of plyers from his father's tool box to squeeze them back onto the bottles, which he hung at different heights. He'd learned from a friend how to heat the bottles and pop the bottoms out with ice water. He had been ten years old, then, so those chimes had been hanging from the veranda of their home for nearly half his life. There were nights they'd cursed the thing, when the wind blew hard from the north, and he had offered to take it down dozens of times. His mother had always refused, though, telling him it was music to her. It had become a tradition for his father to announce his entrance to the house every evening by passing his calloused hand across the bottles, making them sing. There were chips and cracks in almost every one of the six bottles – one for every one of the family. That remained true, still, with the passing of his father and the subsequent arrival of his nephew, Juanito.

Alejandro arrived just as they were ready to leave, and Mateo didn't like the expression on Heidi's face one bit as she showed him her pretty teeth and eyes. The truth was, though, it was good to see a hint of life from his sisters at all since "the day". Heidi was turning into a beautiful young woman, and Mateo knew he'd soon be turning suitors away from her. Corina would be a different kind of problem, since she was clearly slow in her mental capacity. She'd never really advanced from the age of four, and still called him "Teo". Lisbet, also strikingly beautiful with her auburn hair and green eyes, spent all of her time worrying about keeping little Juanito out of trouble to even notice how the young men snapped their necks to get a second look when she passed by. Heidi, the middle sister – she'd be the one to give him his grey hair and worry lines.

He worried about his mother, though. She had never recovered from all of the events of "the day", bringing her husband home in a box, everything she and the girls had suffered, and seeing Mateo covered in blood and having been shot by the same man who had brutalized them. He caught her all too often, just staring off into space, a plate suspended in her hand as though she was a mannequin in a department store. She always seemed to stare in the direction of the coffee fields, as though listening for her husband to stroke the bottles of the chime and brighten the space with his presence. He hoped the change of scenery would do her some good.

His hope of being in Trinidad long before Pomares ascended to Topes de Collantes was only halfway fulfilled. They didn't see his arch enemy, but they were surprised to encounter half a dozen troop trucks, full of young, eager soldiers, at regular intervals along the road, making their way up, probably to prepare for a festive reception of the local hero. He did his best to keep his eyes down, not making contact with any of them. One mortal enemy was more than enough. He warned his sisters to keep their eyes down, and not to provoke them in any way, no matter how loud they whistled and cheered at the sight of females. Heidi giggled at some of the comments after they were out of sight of the trucks, and Lisbet shared a nudge with her sister, mentioning how handsome they looked in their uniforms. Mateo stopped their foolishness with a stern look. Their mother had no reaction, neither positive nor negative. She rocked little Juan, who slept through most of the journey.

Mateo glanced sideways as they passed by the scene of the events of nearly two years earlier. The scar on the road was just a little blip as the wagon crossed over it, and the grass had grown to the same height as the surrounding area where the fire had been. There was just the slightest difference in the green of the new growth. Fire was an excellent way to get rid of unwanted weeds and old growth. He and his father had employed it many times in the coffee plantation to stimulate the growth of the coffee plants. He recalled the all-night conversation he'd had with his father, opening up to him about everything he dreamed about in his life.

At the intersection where the road to Topes met the main highway between Trinidad and Cienfuegos, some sixty miles to the west, Mateo noticed the beginning of construction of some sort of structure, and was surprised to see a pair of serious-looking soldiers step out from the shade of the big tree there and hold their hands up for him to stop. He had never been stopped by any authority before, and he wondered what they could possibly want.

As it turned out, he was supposed to have some sort of identification for his horse, his wagon, and permission for the number of bags of coffee he transported. The official explained the process of registering his wagon, horse and the new government office where he needed to get the permissions necessary to transport and sell coffee. In the future, though, there was to be no coffee sold directly to any individual customers. His coffee would be purchased directly by the state, and redistributed through official channels to where it was needed. When Mateo questioned the process, explaining that he and his father had been selling coffee to the same customers for many years, he was met with an indifferent expression. When he enquired about the price the state would be paying for the coffee, he was met with the officials back. He was done answering questions from a peasant farmer. Even though it was only a dozen kilometers from where they had been interrogated to the entrance to Trinidad, Mateo was greeted twice more by the outstretched arm of a military official, each asking for his papers, which of course he didn't have. One of them detained him for nearly half an hour, for no apparent reason except that he could. Another made a big deal about the fact that none of them carried identification with them. In the future, they were never to travel without their papers.

Their arrival in Trinidad provided more of the same. Movement was restricted at every turn. They were asked where they were going, for what purpose, and who had given them permission. Mateo swallowed his frustration, then his anger, and finally his rage. He was a simple farmer, delivering his wares, as he had done dozens of times before, since he had been a child accompanying his father.

It was when he knocked on the door of his first customer, a sack of fresh coffee on his shoulder that Mateo learned the Cuba he had known all his life was no longer. The small hotel had been a customer for more than ten years, and the proprietor had always invited him in to share a cup of the coffee he brought. This time, though, the door was opened by another person, wearing a uniform. His expression was anything but welcoming. He questioned Mateo's motive for arriving without an appointment or letter of authorization. Mateo searched over his shoulder for the owner, but saw only empty rooms and evidence of things having been packed hastily. He explained politely that he sold coffee to the hotel, and that he came every second week, normally on Saturday, thinking the soldier would make note of it for the future. Instead, he was curtly dismissed, with the explanation that all supplies in the future would be provided by the state-run warehouses, and he should register immediately to sell his coffee to the applicable department there.

The next hotel he arrived at gave him exactly the same story, sending him on his way without a word of welcome. Even the smaller restaurants that consistently purchased half a sack every two weeks advised him they would no longer require his product, since the state had provided them their allotment at a drastically-reduced price. The collective opinion of Mateo's customers was that he had been over-charging them for many years, and finally the state had stepped in to make right the situation. When Mateo asked one of the restaurants to show him the coffee they had received from the state, he was refused.

Finally, after a dozen stops and not one sack of coffee sold, Mateo found directions to the new customer – the state of Sancti Spiritus. He knew the building from its previous life as the local train station – a sprawling warehouse now, with walls being built at intervals to separate different commodities – flour, sugar, vegetables, tobacco, bananas. Each section had a tiny table and chair, attended by a buyer. He found the door marked "coffee", hand-painted in bright red letters. It was under a larger banner announcing that the revolution would provide for all.

When Mateo finally got the attention of the teenaged buyer, he was asked to wait for an hour, because it was now lunch-time. Mateo returned to the wagon, where he and his mother and sisters decided to take advantage of the waiting time to enjoy their own lunch of boiled eggs and chicken sandwiches, while Lisbet changed Juan's diaper and fed him a bottle of milk they had carried with them. Mateo watched the dozens of employees as they congregated in a makeshift cafeteria and laughed and filled themselves with fresh bread and heaps of rice and beans. A younger girl made several rounds with a picture of water and another of coffee. There were bananas and oranges at intervals along the immense table.

It was well over an hour before the young buyer returned to his table, and he seemed in no big hurry to attend Mateo, the only person waiting when he sat down and began to make nonsensical notations on the pad. Finally, he acknowledged Mateo, making sure he understood who would decide when the meeting began and ended. He was a frail young man, besides, and someone whom Mateo could have lifted and thrown a dozen meters. Coffee was not a prioritized commodity, the young man explained to Mateo in a tone someone would use on a student in primary school. The price the state could pay was very low. He handed him a slip of paper, with the approximate price Mateo charged his own customers for a sack of coffee, causing him to wonder how the state could have charged so little to his customers.

"You can unload them over there," the young man stated, waving his arm in the direction of the other sacks along the wall.

"You want me to put my coffee in the same pile as those? Mine is three times the quality. Just look at the color and texture." He showed the buyer the difference, rubbing his coffee between his fingers, showing the chocolate-colored stain that remained. He did the same with the coffee from one of the other sacks, and showed him the green color from picking the beans before their time.

"Thanks for the coffee lesson. Over there." The boy dismissed him and returned to drawing figures in his pad.

Mateo shook his head and decided it wasn't worth his time and effort. If they were going to pay him almost what he received from his customers, and he could make just one delivery, he wouldn't complain. It would be different, not seeing the friends he'd made over the years, but he could still visit them when he had time.

He shook his head each time he passed by the diminutive bean-counter, in every expression of the word. There was no intention to help, no movement to even hold the door open. He just made a little 'x' every time Mateo tossed another of the sacks onto the floor. He'd brought a dozen sacks this time, because he knew the demand would be high, and he wiped the sweat from his neck and forehead in the stifling heat. There was a tub of water nearby, but it wasn't offered to him to wash his hands and face after the last sack was stacked neatly beside the others.

He approached the buyer, who had already counted out the bills to pay him. He handed them to Mateo without a word of thanks for his efforts.

"This is for only one sack of coffee," Mateo corrected him politely, knowing that anyone could make an error.

"I told you the price before you unloaded them," replied the buyer.

"But that was the price for a sack of coffee."

"I showed you the price, and you accepted it, and you unloaded the coffee in the warehouse, so they are now property of the Revolutionary Government of Cuba." He hadn't even looked up from his doodling.

"You can't be serious. I'd like to speak to the person in charge."

"I'm the person in charge of coffee. Anything else?"

"But you can't pay me less for twelve sacks than I sell one sack to my customers!" Mateo tried to be calm and use reason, but he was talking to himself, now. The buyer had exited and headed toward the cafeteria, where he signaled two armed guards to follow him back to his locale.

"You're trespassing on government property. Please vacate." The larger of the two guards made a slight glance down at his rifle, and returned his eyes to Mateo's.

"But this makes no sense," Mateo pleaded. "I can't sell my coffee for less than it costs me to grow. I'll be out of business. How will I feed my family?"

"Your family will be provided for by the generosity of the revolution. Your economic model is gone, now. You won't be getting rich anymore like all of the rest of the slave-driving land-owners."

Mateo stepped back from the shock of what he was hearing. Wealthy, slave-driving? Where was this coming from? No one had ever considered the small farmers up in the mountains to be wealthy, and none of them even had an employee he knew of, let alone a slave. There hadn't been a slave in Cuba that he knew of for more than fifty years. Three of his closest neighbors were Negro men and women. He felt like he'd come down from the mountains and encountered another planet, where all of the people had been forced to drink some concoction that removed their common sense.

The guard made a motion with the barrel of his rifle, signaling Mateo to move on, and the conversation and negotiation were over. He looked at the sacks of coffee that should have provided food and clothing and supplies for his family, and took a mental picture of the buyer and guards for later.

There was some sort of a commotion in the main square as Mateo tried to maneuver his wagon through a gathering crowd. He stood up on the wagon to get a look over their heads, and saw that it was some sort of political function, with a stage set up in the empty lot adjacent to the square. He could see enough to confirm that his enemy, Pomares, was being heralded as the local hero, the man in charge of the new future of Trinidad. As he coaxed his stallion to turn in a circle in the crowded street, he made eye contact with the local hero, and he saw the broad smile form, displaying the new teeth the revolution had already provided its savior. Mateo held the gaze until his wagon had turned on its axis enough to head the opposite way.

"Viva Fidel!" Crowd roaring, repeating. "Viva Cuba!" More roars, more fists pumped in the air. "And VIVA la REVOLUTION!" Frenzied cheering. Women actually crying in joy and emotional outpouring.

Mateo snapped the reins, urging the stallion to pick up its pace, slipping as it already was on the shiny cobble-stones. He felt a need to get Trinidad and the madness behind him, and get back to his farm as soon as he could. The wind that had sounded the chimes at his house during the early morning was picking up, and the clouds to the north and east looked menacing.

Not as menacing, though, as the smile on Pomares' face.

Mateo considered not stopping for the outstretched hand of the same military officer who had detained him only a half dozen hours earlier. He wanted to get back up the mountain before the rain made the already-dangerous slopes even more treacherous. He shook his head when he was asked for his papers by the same person who already knew he had no papers or identification with him. He had to explain where the bags of coffee were, and when he presented the wrinkled piece of paper the buyer had given him with the sum doodled on it, the officer looked at him as though he was insane. He asked where the signatures were, where the seal was from the government warehouse, where even were the date and location. He would be fined for the lack of proper proof. Insult to injury, Mateo kept repeating to himself. First they had stolen his coffee, and now they wanted to make him pay a fine for their own lack of aptitude. The fine he was handed was slightly less than the amount he had been paid for the coffee.

"Could you please sign and date this?" Mateo asked, trying not to sound sarcastic, but failing.

While his sisters unrolled the tarpaulin they used to cover the coffee sacks when it rained, Mateo waited for the official to communicate with someone on his radio before allowing them to continue on their way. He was advised he would need to wait until a procession passed of officials on their way up to Topes de Collantes. Having pulled the wagon into a narrow approach and under the branches of an overhanging tree, they were somewhat camouflaged from the main roadway, so when the caravan of Jeeps and trucks passed by them, hardly a head turned in their direction. Mateo couldn't mistake seeing Pomares in the back seat of one of the lead Jeeps as they roared past at high speed. So much for being home before the party started.

The rain came as they turned off the main road to head up the slope toward Topes, and the child cried from the cold, or the dark, or something else that bothered him. Mateo imagined to himself that it was from the shame of who his biological father was, and silently hoped little Juan would cry himself to sleep. The ascent was slow but steady. The stallion was strong, and wanted to go faster than Mateo allowed it. He'd helped clean up the remains of people who'd hurried up the mountain.

When they finally pulled into their own gravel entrance, the festivities were winding down. Alejandro had milked the cow, fed the animals, and gathered the chickens and ducks in for the night. He was anxious to get to the town square to catch the last of the party, and hardly took time to say hello to Mateo and his sisters before racing down the main road. Heidi looked toward Mateo, seeking permission, but found none. She frowned and led Corina to their bedroom, while Lisbet fired up the kerosene stove to prepare water for their baths. Mateo's mother sat on the long bench under the wind chime, listening to the far-off music and revelry. Mateo brushed down the stallion, after pulling off the harness and storing it in the barn.

Just knowing the bastard was in the same part of the world made his blood boil, and he felt his hands shake as he brushed the stallion's powerful flank, counting out loud as was his habit. Five hundred strokes in total. It was nearly midnight when he closed the gate behind the horse, and stretched his arms and neck until he felt muscles and bones snap into their original places. He could have slept standing up, he was so exhausted from the events of the day. He made a mental note of some of the repairs awaiting him for the morning, just a few hours away. He was surprised to see his mother, still sitting in the same position on the porch when he arrived at the house. Her eyes were wide open, still looking toward the center of town, even though it was hidden behind two long curves in the road, some three miles to the east of them.

"He's down there right now," she said, almost a whisper.

"It's behind us, now, Mom," Mateo comforted her, lying.

"It'll be behind me when he's in the ground, Mateo." The look in her eyes told him she meant exactly what she was saying. He wondered if it was possible she hated Pomares even more than he did. After all, she was their mother – he was just their older brother.

"He'll pay, Mother," he tried to assure her. "It's just not the right time."

When he woke up, he was surprised to see his sisters and mother all standing beside his bed. He sprang to a seated position, shaking himself to the present. He'd only hit the stiff straw mattress four hours earlier. Corina couldn't contain herself, and shouted "happy birthday" first, followed by the rest of the girls, and little Juan even chimed in, mimicking the girls. His mother had prepared his favorite breakfast of eggs and fried pork. He could hardly believe he was only nineteen years old. He felt like a forty-year-old, tied by responsibility and obligation to his mother and sisters. He hadn't remembered it was his birthday the night before when he'd convinced his mother to come inside and try to sleep sometime after one in the morning.

It was Lisbet who called him outside after breakfast. She had been worried about him for some time. The source of her worry was his insistence in thinking about the rest of them all of the time, and never once about his own happiness or future. She'd done some preliminary scouting, and had a surprise for him, but she wanted him to have an open mind about it, before she presented her "birthday gift". Naturally, Mateo scoffed at the idea, making the excuse that there wasn't time for that sort of nonsense. Lisbet caught the discoloration on his sunbaked cheeks, and knew she'd been right.

After milking the cow and taking care of the rest of the animals, Mateo mended the broken post at the corner of the corral that he had noticed the previous evening, and tightened the top strand of the barbed wire fence where the cow had stretched it in her quest for the greener grass on the other side. His mother insisted he have a bath and shave for the birthday lunch she'd prepared, and even though he resisted, citing the hours of work still ahead weeding the coffee plants, he finally agreed.

Gladys was her name, Lisbet had told him when he walked out of the bathroom and into the ambush. He knew who she was, actually. She lived only a couple of farms to the east, next to the Negro family with the nine children. But she was only a kid, and he gave Lisbet a look that indicated her idea had been a failure, because he wasn't interested in having another child around the house. Gladys, on the other hand, seemed completely taken by the tall and handsome Mateo. Hormones, he decided. How old could she be, anyway? Twelve?

She was nearly fifteen, he was corrected by Lisbet when he finally got her alone. Their mother had been fifteen when she married their father, she reminded him. Most importantly, she liked him, and that was no small feat, given his workaholic nature and lack of personal skills. Being between Lisbet and Heidi in age had made Gladys their closest friend in the community, and the only person in the world they had ever confided in as to the events of "the day". She was one of the few in the community not to have fallen over themselves to welcome Pomares back the previous evening.

They ate together at the table, laughed at the poor excuse for a cake the girls had managed to bake on the stove, and Mateo allowed himself a sliver of light to enter the darkness in his heart. Gladys wasn't pretty like his sisters Lisbet and Heidi. She was shorter than either of them, and heavier than he would find attractive. She had a healthy laugh, though, and good manners. She insisted on helping to clean up the table, and made a point of carrying his dishes. It was obvious there had been some serious strategizing between the girls, and her visit hadn't been as spontaneous as they'd let on. When Gladys had reached past his shoulder to pick up his plate and knife and fork, he noted the perfume. Up in the mountains, at least, people didn't put on perfume for a chance visit that turned into an invitation to a meal. Mateo hauled Juan onto his lap, clapping his big calloused hands over the child's as he repeated the parts he remembered of the birthday song.

The following day, Mateo called on Gladys' parents, explaining to them that he planned to marry their daughter after her fifteenth birthday. All he had left to offer was a good horse and a few pigs, but he promised he would always take care of her. They were older, and had only managed one child, so they agreed to accept Mateo's promise. It hadn't hurt his cause that Mateo's father had helped them to bury their parents when they'd succumbed to a particularly nasty flu only a few years earlier.

In the months before Gladys' fifteenth birthday, Mateo continued his daily routine of work, exercise, counting and taking care of his sisters and mother. What he learned during that time was that he had been singled out in the community as a trouble-maker, and there were certain factions conspiring against him. He'd learned, for example, a neighbor who had sold coffee to the same young buyer on the same day received more than four times the price Mateo had been paid, and for significantly lower quality coffee. The famous quota books that had been distributed to every man, woman and child in the community were slightly different from the ones he and his family had received. There were several fewer items in his and his sisters' books than in those of Gladys and her family. Supposedly, for the less fortunate like his sister Corina, there were programs and assistance from the state, since she was incapable of contributing or studying. In their case, they were told there was no such help.

It turned out, being a decorated war hero, with the facial scars to prove his dedication to the cause, gave Pomares more credibility. History books were written by the victors, as they said, and Mateo had recently heard how their fearless new leader had been brutally attacked by several members of the Batista militia, where he'd lost several teeth and had his jaw broken. He displayed the medal proudly on his uniform. People in Mateo's own community, and most specifically those who had found new jobs and added benefits from their relationship to Pomares, suddenly had been witness to his acts of bravery like the one that left him scarred for life, and three Batista soldiers dead. One of those witnesses, coincidently, was one of the boys who had run home to get help the day Mateo had confronted Pomares. Manolo Aguila was the new leader of the local CDR, Committee for the Defense of the Revolution, also responsible for the distribution of the quota books. The other boy, Juan Carlos Gonzalez, enjoyed a nice salary and the benefits that went along with his assignment as liaison to Pomares for the community. This basically meant listening to every conversation he could, and reporting anything that needed to be dealt with to ensure the people in power stayed there. Mateo's fist was beginning to take on super powers, it seemed. His single punch had now killed three Batista soldiers, and elevated another three school dropouts into positions of wealth and influence while his own family dropped in status every day.

Gladys turned fifteen, and Mateo's sisters spent the morning helping her prepare for the ceremony that would be held at her parents' home. They braided her long hair and Heidi crushed some wild flowers and made a nice pinkish eye shadow. Corina had been in charge of the bouquet, and had found enough roses of different colors to make Gladys', a white rose for Mateo to pin to his shirt, and smaller arrangements for each of the sisters and her and Gladys' mother. Mateo's mother spent the morning sewing buttons she had salvaged from two of Mateo's older shirts onto the guayabera she had made from the whitest bed sheet they had left.

Mateo, as always, had been in the barn before the sun came up, milking the cow and feeding the horses and mules and other animals. The beasts had a way of reminding him that one day was no more special than the last to them. They needed food and water and daily attention. There were no vacation days on the farm. The fifteen minutes of milking the cow, though, did afford him time to let his thoughts wander to the fact he was going to be a married man within a few hours, and aside from the fact it meant another person he would be responsible for, he felt a tingle of nerves and anticipation at the thought of the physical part of having a wife. He was nearly twenty years old, but anything resembling a normal youth and teenaged life had been skipped over by the events of his life. He'd never even been on a single date before he met Gladys, and had never even been one with her, either. He had only kissed her on the cheek when they'd visited on the few occasions he'd stopped at her parents' home regarding matters of coffee. He liked how she blushed so obviously whenever they

had been in the same room. She'd never had
another boyfriend, either. He thought about how
his sisters had giggled as they moved their mother's
things out of the only bedroom with a wall
separating it from the other sleeping areas. They'd
even strung up a curtain over the open doorway,
making it as private as it could be.

The ceremony had been planned for five in the
afternoon, to allow Mateo time with the coffee
plants in need of attention, and before the evening
chores. Aside from Gladys' parents, she had
invited her best friend from school and two cousins.
Mateo counted the heads for the meal, and decided
two of the geese and three good-sized chickens
would assure everyone left with full bellies. The
weather had conspired against them, though, and an
unseasonable drizzle forced him to do the killing
and dressing of the birds under the giant tree on the
way down to the creek in the pasture. He was
nearly an hour later than he'd wanted to be when he
carried the carcasses to the outdoor kitchen and
handed them off to Lisbet and his mother. He saw
the mountain of rice and beans they'd already
cleaned and the size of the pots they'd be prepared
in, and just shook his head. So much work for
everyone else didn't sit well with Mateo, but he
knew it was just the way things were. He could do
many things, but cooking was not one of those. He
was relieved to see Gladys' mother and one of her
female cousins arrive with bread and plates and
glasses in hand. Gladys, Heidi and Corina were at
her house spending the day out of sight of Mateo.

He was glad to have the coffee plants to keep him busy. This kind of fuss and bother were uncomfortable to Mateo. He didn't need to consult any clock to know he was already behind, and said a brief and polite greeting to his future mother-in-law, grabbed two bananas and half a loaf of bread for breakfast, and strode off toward the barn where the mule would be finishing its own morning meal.

"Don't be late," his mother warned him, a proud smile on her face.

"Late for what?" Mateo winked back at her. He noticed his father's old dress shoes had been polished and repaired. Rebuilt, more like it, since Mateo's feet were two sizes larger than his father's had been. His mother had taken them to the local shoe maker who had spliced in a piece of leather to the back seams and had moved the heals an inch to the rear. The leather he'd added had a distinctly blue color, compared to the black of his father's shoes, but there had been no time to choose. They looked odd, to say the least, but getting married in his tall rubber work boots was the alternative. He chuckled to himself that he had something, old, new, borrowed and blue, all rolled into one. That had to be a good omen.

Up on the steep slopes where the coffee plants were, Mateo confirmed his suspicions of the previous week – there had been someone else present recently, and they hadn't been there to help weed. Broken branches and trampled sections from the hooves of shod horses up and down almost every row of plants were easy to confirm. Whoever had been there, they hadn't been very careful to hide their presence. Mateo noted that the ripest beans were still hanging from the branches, so it hadn't been anyone looking to steal his coffee – at least not someone who knew the business. He spent the first few hours acting like a doctor who'd come across a bus crash, rushing from one victim to the next, making the decision as to which could be saved, and which one to just end its suffering. As he snipped the broken branches, he harvested what ripe beans he could from them, and placed them into the rows to serve as mulch for the surviving ones. He calculated as he went that at least ten percent of the plants had suffered severe damage. He and his father had battled insect attacks, worms, birds, and drought, but none had been as devastating as two or three men on horseback. Aside from everything else, now, he'd need to spend more time guarding his crops. He made a mental note to ask his father-in-law to check for the same in his crop of coffee, just a few kilometers from Mateo's. He thanked God silently that his father hadn't seen the destruction – it had taken him years to clear the steep slopes, sow and nurture forty thousand plants, make waterways, access routes for the mules. It had all been a labor of love, building a future for his family. Up until the previous week, there had never been a single branch broken out of carelessness, not a bean wasted. Mateo had learned from his father to treat the coffee like a cherished family member, because that's what it was for them.

He worked and fixed, plant after plant, row after row. He'd set his internal alarm for four o'clock, time to get home and washed and into his fancy clothes for the wedding. He knew he'd left more work to his mother and sisters than he would have liked, but the coffee was what kept them all fed and clothed. He had already hit his own snooze button three times before he finally looked up from the row he'd been tending to. There was so much more to do, but now he'd barely have time to wash himself and comb his hair by five o'clock if he rushed the mule home. The light rain would make it impossible to hurry, though. Even the sure-footed mule needed to keep its wits about it not to lose footing where the clay seeped onto the rocky trail. Mateo had fallen himself, once, earlier in the day, and had a nasty bruise on his right thigh to show for it. His regular limp from his left foot was off-set with the new pain on his right side. A fine figure of a man, he thought to himself as he brushed under a tree branch, showering himself and the mule with the accumulated water on the leaves. The good news was he'd be half-showered by the time he arrived.

The clouds rested on the slopes of the mountain, making day into near-dusk by the time Mateo wiped the mule down and tossed the meager sack of coffee he'd salvaged into the sorting bin where he prepared and roasted the coffee. He would need to take the time to pick the ripe beans in the next couple of days, before continuing the rescue efforts.

He was surprised not to see anyone outside cooking when he finally limped to the house. No music, either, which was strange for his sisters. If there was no electricity to use the old transistor radio, they would normally be singing and dancing, especially on an occasion like this one. Mateo put on his party face, stroked the bottles of the chime into service, and burst through the front door, certain he was being set up for a surprise greeting.

His surprise was to find the house full, but not with friends or family. His mother and sisters sat at the table, tears in their eyes, mouths closed, obviously not by their choice. Little Juan had his face buried in Lisbet's chest. He counted seven armed militia, none more than twenty-five years old, standing at attention. From the bedroom, Mateo heard footsteps. The curtain parted to reveal Pomares, in full uniform, sporting a grin from his new set of teeth.

Mateo's hand reached for his knife in his pocket, but he changed his mind when he saw the rifles raise, not in his own direction, but that of his mother and sisters. He'd wanted to have Pomares within reach since "the day", and would have torn him limb from limb the first chance he got, but he knew this wasn't the opportunity he'd been waiting for.

"There's a new operative from Havana," began Pomares, in his most authoritative voice. "The Commandant has ordered us to reclaim the land unjustly held by the supporters of the Batista regime. The Committee for the Defense of the

Revolution has decried this to be the most obvious example."

Mateo's blood boiled. "So the horses trampling the coffee plants are yours?"

"Not mine, but Revolutionary, none-the-less."

"Then the Revolution will pay me for the damages, I assume?" Mateo tried to control his hatred, but felt his body shaking with rage and futility.

"It won't be necessary, Mateo, old friend." He pronounced the last two words as though he was talking to a cherished member of his family at a church ceremony. "The coffee plants will be well cared for by their rightful owners."

Mateo took a step forward, with the immediate reaction of seven barrels being trained on his heart. "Who will those rightful owners be?"

"The true owners of all of the land in Cuba – the Cuban working class."

"But I'm the Cuban working class!" Mateo shouted.

Pomares couldn't contain himself any longer. He laughed out loud. "You, sir, are what we fought this revolution about. To take Cuba back from the wealthy and put it back in the hands of the poor." He stared straight at Lisbet. "And to provide a proper moral standard for the people, where children won't be born out of wedlock, like that young man over there. Lisbet made a sound, as though she were about to speak, but swallowed her words in a whimper. "As the man of the house, you will be taken to a reform area, while we provide a suitable place for your mother and sisters in Trinidad."

Mateo couldn't believe what he was hearing. Taken? Reformed? This was madness.

"But he's only a boy!" Mateo's mother muttered.

"He looks like a pretty big man to me," Pomares countered, motioning for the militia to tie Mateo's hands behind his back and remove his knife.

"Put the guns down, and let's find out, just you and me." Mateo spit the words at Pomares, staring into his eyes, noting the fear of the child. "You and all of the rest of these idiots together, if you prefer." Mateo saw Pomares nod his head toward the closest soldier, and saw the butt of the rifle rise beside his head, and then nothing.

PART FIVE

Mateo woke up with a splitting headache and the pain of several other impacts to his body, from either rifle butts or army boots, he wasn't sure. He felt the dried blood from his nose. It was still almost dark – he had no idea where he was, but he knew it was four-forty-eight in the morning. His internal clock was still functioning, he confirmed. The small amount of light that came from the adjoining room outlined the narrow opening from the solid metal door. There were no windows, and he heard no external sounds, causing him to believe he was in an internal room of a large building. He heard movement and labored breathing from the opposite side of the room, and felt his way along the wall until he found the source. It was the flower that let him know who the body belonged to. When he pulled him onto his back, Mateo felt a flattened rose pinned to his chest. It took a few seconds to realize it was his father-in-law-to-be, Roberto Ramirez, since the face was all but unrecognizable. As his eyes adjusted to the semi-darkness, he cradled the other man's head in his lap. He got no response from calling his name, and could see nothing of recognition in his half-closed eyes. His first reaction was to call out for help, but he nearly coughed himself unconscious when he tried to raise his voice.

As he leaned back against the cold concrete wall, trying to push through the nausea and all of the pain from so many parts of his head and body, he felt Mr. Ramirez' back arch suddenly until his entire body was supported by his feet and neck, followed by an uncontrollable seizure. Then nothing more. He collapsed like a giant rag doll, his head still on Mateo's lap, and stopped the labored breathing that had been the beacon that led Mateo to him.

Mateo could see the outline of the door clearly enough to make his way there, and he pounded on it for someone to come and help. His fists bled and his voice was nothing more than a whisper, but no one came to the rescue of his cell-mate. Finally, all that was left was to comfort the man and promise to take care of his only daughter. Mateo closed Mr. Ramirez' eyes that seemed to have kept staring at him with the questioning look of 'why'. He threw his head back against the rough block wall and let out a long wail that sounded more animal than human.

It wasn't until sometime the following morning when the guards got around to removing Mr. Ramirez' body, and not with any modicum of sensitivity. Mateo took more care in cleaning out the stalls of his barn than the four men did hauling a person's body outside where he heard the thud when he was tossed onto a wagon of some sort to be discarded far enough away so as not to foul their quarters. Apparently filth like Mateo and Mr. Ramirez didn't merit a dignified funeral service. The family would be told of the death when they arrived in a month for their first approved visit.

The psychological punishment began immediately afterward. Mateo, an unusually large man, had always had an appropriately large appetite, and with his strenuous exercise regimen, his body required constant and quality nutrition, something it never lacked on the farm. His first meal after nearly twenty-four hours in custody was a plate of chicken bones that had been chewed clean by the guard moments before, while Mateo was forced to watch. The guard devoured an entire chicken, with a side plate of rice and beans, enjoying the feast and covering his face and fingers with the excess. He drank two large glasses of ice-cold water, pouring the last of the second glass on the floor, taking care to stomp the two remaining chunks of ice. From a filthy basin beside the door, he scraped the bottom with an empty glass, making sure not to leave the slime and bird excrement, and to add to the show, he spit into it, while looking Mateo in the eyes all the while. Careful not to get close enough for Mateo to reach him, he not-so-accidently let the bones fall onto the floor of the cell, and set the glass down carefully, so as not to spill a drop of the putrid liquid.

"Bon appetite," the guard hissed in his best French accent. Mateo ignored his poor attempt at humor. He also ignored the chicken bones and swamp water, relying on his physical reserves. Tomorrow would be better, he reasoned.

Unfortunately, every tomorrow was worse than the previous day, and the treatment only increased its inhumanity. A week after his arrival, and Mateo dreamed of the chicken bones and filthy water, compared to what they were tossing into his cell. Had it not been for the trickle of water down a crack in the wall, he'd have perished already from dehydration. On the fourth night, he heard other prisoners being tossed into an adjoining cell, but he remained alone. Clearly, due to his history with a certain military officer, he was receiving the five star royal treatment.

Two weeks after arrival, and already weaker than he could ever remember being, he heard the sound of women and children outside. Visiting day. His spirits soared. Surely he would have at least a few minutes with his wife-to-be and mother and sisters. He tried to put on his best face for their visit. It wasn't long before he heard familiar voices – it was his mother's he recognized first, but she was clearly crying and in distress. He pressed himself against the door, trying to hear the conversation, but all he could gather was that they were sending her home. It couldn't be… he could hear the sounds of reuniting families from the next cell, and was tortured by the smells of food they had brought the other prisoners. There was his wife-to-be's voice, also crying, pleading with the guard to let her see Mateo. Finally, he heard the voices trail off as the women were escorted from the premises.

That evening, Mateo recognized the aluminum pot he used to take up to the coffee plantation with his warm lunch. One of the guards opened the door to his cell, making a show of enjoying the taste of the rice and pork and beans he heaped into his mouth from the pot. When he couldn't take anymore, he pretended to accidentally drop it, spilling the remainder onto the floor, where a pair of the dogs that had made the prison home swooped in to gobble every grain of rice, growling and snarling at each other. Mateo's stomach heaved from the anticipation, and he forced the vomit back into his stomach that had climbed up to the back of his throat.

For the first time since he'd arrived, Mateo cried from the pain of the hunger and from being so close to seeing his mother and fiancé, and having had that ripped from him as well. He tried to push the pain back and sleep, but his internal clock seemed to have increased its volume to a deafening roar. The seconds throbbed in his brain, the minutes became daggers and the hours ripped him limb from limb like the ancient torture devices. He screamed at himself to stop the clock, to let him die in silence.

A few nights later, he tasted for the first time what would become a staple for Mateo for the coming years. Rice with hair on the top and a putrid water underneath. Some of the prisoners from the next cell had received care packages of arroz congris, the famous rice and black bean dish famous throughout Cuba. Since there was no refrigeration for the prisoners, food lasted only a day at most with the heat and humidity up in the mountains. The rice began to taste bad by the second night, and by the third, it began to smell so foul that the prisoners asked the guards to remove it so they could sleep without the odor. The guards found it more amusing to toss it into Mateo's cell, instead. By the time it landed in his cell, it was already well putrefied, and the dried rice on top had woven itself into a greyish/brown cake of hairy mush, while the oily liquid from the bottom of the pot oozed from under the mass. Mateo tried to remember how much he loved the congris, fresh and hot when he returned from the evening chores. He knew if he didn't eat something, he would die of starvation. Already weak from three days with scarcely a bite of food, he held his nose to dull the smell, and to trick his taste buds enough to swallow. He had managed to save enough water in a discarded paper he'd rolled into a cone that he could chase the filth down his throat. There wouldn't have been enough water in the creek that flowed through his pasture to have masked the taste, though, and his stomach rejected the first few attempts, retching involuntarily. Finally, after the third attempt, he kept it down, and ate the entire bowlful.

That night, Mateo slept without the pain of an empty stomach, and vowed to do whatever it took to keep himself alive. He had too many reasons not to let them win – his mother and sisters, first, then his wife-to-be, and finally his burning need to tear Ruben Pomares into tiny pieces. And to get his farm back.

The following morning, he learned there was another benefit to the rotten rice – three rats had ventured in through whatever crevice they came from and were so busy gorging on the filthy liquid that two of them were surprised by Mateo's bare feet as they came down on them. He would learn how to stomach raw rat meat, too. When the guard opened the door to toss in the scraps from the others' breakfast, he was visibly sickened by the sight of the entrails of the rats, and the empty space on the floor where he'd tossed the rice the previous evening. If they planned to wage a psychological war against him, Mateo intended to launch his own offensive.

Another month passed, and Mateo continued to find ways to survive, both physically and mentally. He used his internal clock to maintain a strict and disciplined routine. At five-fifteen in the morning, he would force himself to get up, clean himself as best he could with the scarce amount of water he could save from the trickle, and count the steps it would have taken him to reach his barn to feed and milk the two cows, and he would mime the action of tossing grain and leftover rice from the family's evening meal to the imaginary chickens. He would even gather the imaginary eggs. He expanded his twelve-foot-by-twelve-foot cell into the size of his farm, walking in circles until he had reached his coffee plantation, seeing the plants in his mind's eye, and even talking to them, willing them to grow strong and fruitful. The banana and orange peels that were tossed into his cell for breakfast became the ham and eggs his sisters shared with him after chores. He always left enough for the never-ending supply of rats, and could prepare and devour one in record time, after a few weeks passed. He even felt strong enough to resume a modified exercise program, mostly consisting of push-ups and stomach crunches.

He heard his mother and Gladys outside again, with the other visitors, and heard them pleading to be allowed to see him. Though he seethed with anger and the pain of them being so near, he knew he couldn't allow the bastards to torture them. He summoned his courage and strength, and hollered through the space under the door. "I'm okay, Momma! Don't worry about me. Take care of Gladys and my sisters and little Juanito. I'll be home soon..." He knew that was a lie, but he wanted the torture to end. He knew it must have been hard enough for his mother to find food for his wife and sisters, let alone bringing more to him. It was too much of a sacrifice to find a way to come all the way up the mountain, only to have the food eaten by the guards. He'd have another feast of hairy rice within a couple of days.

There were many who found solitary confinement to be one more form of torture, but Mateo didn't mind at all. He was happy that his early-morning routines and exercise habits didn't bother anyone else. His life on the farm was a solitary one, and especially after the death of his father. He got up before anyone else in the house stirred, and seldom came in from the barn to rest without finding his mother and sisters and nephew fast asleep. When he saw the bricks and cement carried into his cell, he assumed it was to be divided, so more prisoners could be accommodated. He was only partially right. Some psychological expert in Havana had too much time on his hands, and started to send out messages about how the conditions of the prisoners was much too comfortable for people so despicably evil.

Surely that psychologist had relocated to one of the massive mansions along Fifth Avenue in Havana, and ate his weight in beef and fresh fruit and vegetables every day. Mateo, the evil coffee plantation owner, had it far too good in his twelve foot square cell with the dirt floor and no bathroom. It was only when he saw the size of the compartment that was being built that he realized they weren't dividing his cell in two, or even four equal parts. They were making him his own personal torture chamber. The inside measurements were only two feet wide by four feet in length – too short to lie down in, and not high enough to stand up to his full height. He would need to either kneel or sit with his knees bent to his chest. Mateo was to be the human guinea pig for the new government toy – political prisoners. He was officially one of the first prisoners, and since slavery had been abolished, it was a new opportunity to exercise total control over another human being.

Twenty hours a day, Mateo was forced to sit or kneel in uncomfortable positions, especially for such a large man. This time, all of the blocks were sealed tightly, so there would be no nourishing rats any longer. Mateo closed his eyes in the darkness, and opened his mind. He continued with his morning routine of feeding his invisible animals, walking to the coffee plantation, smelling the plants and tasting the ripe beans. He mentally washed himself in the basin outside on the front, and he could hear the chime that he stroked on his way in for dinner where his mother and sisters waited for him with their clean clothes and warm smiles.

When they let him out for two hours, twice a day, he made a show of looking like he'd just come from an afternoon at the beach. Even though he ached for a drink of water, he always waited until the guard had closed the main door before he twisted his back into shape and hobbled to the crack in the wall, slurping all he could of the brownish liquid. If there was nothing but the handful of sour rice or potato broth, he imagined it was a feast of roasted pork. If it was after visiting day, he would savor the taste of the hairy rice and beans, immune to the foul taste, long ago.

It was only when his mind wandered to his fiancé and family that the melancholy would overtake him. He knew they had to be struggling, just to stay alive, and yet his mother never failed to send a loaf of bread and fresh beans and rice, knowing full well he would never taste them.

As quickly as he could, he would push those thoughts aside, replacing them with the anticipation of seeing them all again one day. His internal clock had a calendar attached to it, and he counted the days, weeks and months, hoping against hope that even though there had never been a trial, his sentence might have an expiration date.

PART SIX

It hadn't been a year, then, because that anniversary had come and gone. He could reset his goal at two years. That was surely long enough for any man to suffer for not having done anything at all except defend the honor of his kid sister against the wrong person.

It hardly made a difference to Mateo, but for the others in the cells beside him, the news they were being transferred to a larger facility hundreds of miles away was devastating. They all lived for their monthly care packages and the few minutes they were allowed to see their loved ones face to face. For Mateo, it was a small relief to know his mother wouldn't waste her precious money and time to send food he never saw. It was one more loaf of bread for them.

He knew he had been spared the fate of so many of Batista's officers, who had been publically and humiliatingly shot by firing squad during the early months after the triumph of the revolution. Their first order of business had been to disarm the potential retaliation forces, and to rid the island of any military knowledge. Fidel's frequent and never-ending speeches were played ad nauseam on the radio stations and the newly-formed television channel. All Fidel, all the time. Anyone who was conscious learned of the benevolence of the Revolutionary Forces, and of the dangers of associating with those who might conspire against them, because they were surely working with the Imperialist devil to the north, who was bent on attacking them and taking away all of the advances they were making toward the perfect state of Socialism.

And Mateo continued to defy them by finding ways to overcome whatever new obstacle was put in front of him. If he couldn't stand up and walk around his cell, he would squat and kneel and stand on his head if he had to. He would send his mind to his farm while his body dealt with the discomfort or pain or the constant hunger. A cockroach tasted like a fresh egg from his best hen, if he put his mind in the right place. When he couldn't converse with his fellow prisoners, or even the guards, he would have conversations with his mother and sisters and even his wife-to-be, although he scarcely had time to know what opinions Gladys had about anything in the world. He invented her opinions, and had little arguments with her over trivial things like how many children they wanted to have, what colors to paint the bedrooms, what remedy was best to fight a fever.

Finally they were placed in trucks that would take them to another truck that would take them to the boat that crossed the small straight that led to the Isle of Youth, only now they weren't allowed to call it the Isle of Youth, because the name had been changed to the Isle of Pinos. When Mateo was guided forcefully from his solitary cell to the giant Russian truck, he saw some of his old neighbors for the first time, even though many of them had been prisoners nearly as long as he had. He could scarcely believe he'd been in prison nearly two years, already, and had not seen another person, other than the guards who threw him the scraps they called food. To Mateo, these weren't really people, because people had their own thoughts and ideas, and treated others as they hoped to be treated in return.

What came as a surprise to Mateo was to learn that he was something of a celebrity among the fastest-growing segment of the population in Cuba – political prisoners. So far as anyone could tell, Mateo was the longest-surviving of the prisoners anywhere on the island, having been the first to be divested of his land and animals, and had served as the model for the thousands of others after him. As often happens, the overheard stories of how he stoically accepted every new method of punishment had filtered through the local prison, and been exaggerated dramatically when one inmate had been transferred to another, or from the stories the others told their wives or family members who were allowed to visit them. Mateo was a big man, but he was much bigger by the time the stories bounced around the country. In his own cell, he had caught and killed rats and eaten them. By the third edition two provinces away, he had bitten the heads off of live rats in front of the guards. If he spent a week in the cramped box, it became a month. If four guards had physically forced him to remove his clothes, it became eight. The fact that Mateo was the first prisoner to defy the orders to wear a blue prisoner uniform, preferring to be naked, gave strength to the thousands after him, all from the first wave of prisoners, to declare their opposition to accept the dress code. Those who were imprisoned after the first year of the revolution were considered different from the originals. Most of the "new" bunch had actually stood up against the new regimen, publically voicing their opposition. The first generation hadn't had the opportunity to taste the revolution before their liberty was taken from them for their crime of owning a piece of land, or a successful business. If they had shown the least amount of support for Batista's defense, no matter if they'd given the same support to Castro's, the justification was swift and indefensible. Opportunities for vengeance abounded.

The new prison on the Isle of Pinos was massive, and looked more like a gigantic hog-farming operation than a prison. Long, narrow buildings with metal roofs that made them into ovens during the heat of the day, stretched for as far as the eye could see. There were no divisions inside of them. The men lived like so many chickens, sleeping on dirt floors, urinating and defecating in the designated corner of each barrack. Seniority within each warehouse dictated the living arrangements – the longer the time served, the further away from the "bathroom" facilities. Newcomers had to sleep next to the foul area, doing their best to cover the filth with dirt and sand they scraped from the rest of the unit. They were severely punished for being caught picking up dirt from the yard during their limited time outside every day.

Mateo was received as a returning war hero when he stepped into the prison for the first time. The collective cheering of thousands of prisoners startled him as much as it did the officials in charge of the prison. The first-generation prisoners, obvious by their lack of blue prison garb, made a line to shake his hand and clap his back as he found his legs again after so many hours of sitting on trucks and the boat across the strait. Mateo's eyes moistened at the unexpected and, in his mind, undeserved notoriety. He recognized a few faces among the thousands, although most were only shadows of the strong men he had known. Lucky for him there were no mirrors, or he would have scarcely recognized himself, either.

He was escorted by the apparent leaders of the prisoners to the most comfortable area of the barrack he'd been assigned to. One of these men had obviously given up his place for Mateo. There had been some time to prepare for the arrival of the legend who Mateo had been transformed into through stories and exaggeration. A few grains of rice from a hundred people made for a feast for him. He could easily have eaten all of it, and half a dozen heaping plates more just like it, but Mateo couldn't begin to enjoy gorging on the fresh rice while others watched him. He respectfully ate a third of it, reveling in the sensation of eating something that hadn't been left in the sun for two days before being served to him. He had almost forgotten the taste, but it came back to him quickly, his glands opening up as he hesitated to swallow, wanting the flavor to stay with him as long as possible. Could it possibly have been years since he'd eaten a plate of rice prepared by his loving family?

There would be no sleep for Mateo the first night. Too many people had waited for the opportunity to file past him and pay him their respects. Anyone who had even a remote connection to him – a friend of a distant relative, another coffee plantation owner, someone who had spent time in the same small prison in Topes de Collantes – all wanted to announce their potentially higher position in the prison hierarchy, searching Mateo's eyes for some sign of recognition that might be used to their advantage. Even if it just moved them a few yards further from the filth and stench of the bathroom corner – they would take any morsel they could get.

When the line finally subsided, Mateo closed his eyes and breathed. His nostrils filtered out the filth of the makeshift bathrooms, and the stench of hundreds of men who hadn't bathed properly in months, in inhumanly hot conditions. He searched his memory to find something that would help him to forget where he was. There were no coffee plantations in this part of the island, but he found the scent of horses – not close enough, but somewhere near. Of all of the animals on his farm, he most loved the smell of his horses, and it made him wonder where they were now. If they hadn't been butchered for meat for the army, they'd be pulling some sort of wagon for the benefit of the revolution. Unfortunately, he had trained them well, so they would be of significant value to someone. He picked up the smell of the smoke from a coal fire, probably from the guard house, where there would be fresh meat and vegetables on their table. Mateo had gone so long without tasting meat he wasn't sure he would recognize it anymore. The guards often cooked meat outdoors, when the breeze carried the assault on the sensory preceptors of the prisoners. Some of them actually gagged or vomited from the smell of fresh meat. The truth was, for Mateo, it wasn't meat or fresh vegetables or fruit that he missed most – it was ice. His favorite thing in the world was to drink all of his beverages in a glass filled with ice. In his house the freezer of the old Russian "apparatus", as they called it, was always crammed with containers of ice of every size and shape. If he went out to his coffee plantation for a day of work, he wrapped two litre bottles of ice in a thick towel to ensure he would never drink water that wasn't ice cold. Here in the prisons, it wasn't the foul smell, or the color of the water that turned his stomach. It was the temperature of it. He would never let on to the guards who purposely spilled their heaping plates of food on the ground outside of the barracks, but it was never the wasting of good food that bothered him. It was the condensation on the sides of their glasses of whatever they happened to be drinking that told him their beverage was cold.

After a fitful night of tossing on a different surface than his body had become accustomed to, Mateo awoke to a new menace from their captors. There had been some rumors from the American invaders who had failed so miserably at the Bay of Pigs invasion. Some said they might try to help the prisoners escape to mount another internal offensive. Others insisted there were actually Americans spies who had infiltrated the prisons to work from the inside. It was the standing joke at meal-times that not many Yankees would actually volunteer to eat the slop they were served here, so they'd want to act fast. There was unusual activity outside the walls of the barracks, with digging and scraping and wires being buried in shallow trenches. The activity continued for several days before someone got the message that explosives had been strategically installed around the prison so that if there was any attempt to infiltrate or sabotage the facilities, there wouldn't be anything or anyone left to rescue.

The truth was, the disaster that was the "Bay of Pigs" invasion had no further motives. There was no plan to rescue prisoners, and no plan to repeat the fiasco. Washington had decided they would play their other cards – economic isolation. Fidel would give up and fly away to some island far away as soon as he realized he couldn't sell his cigars to the rich Yankees. Order would be restored. Casinos would reopen, and the parties would pick up where they left off. Cubans who had fled the island with their suitcases filled with money would come back to their mansions and Cuba would be Cuba again.

PART SEVEN

When it became evident that the threats of foreign intervention had been nothing but speculation and wishful thinking by some starry-eyed prisoners, the suggestions began that the explosives be removed. The guards seemed to enjoy this new form of mental terrorism, though, and threats to set off one or two of the explosives sent several prisoners over their limit of mental sanity. There wasn't room in the barracks to leave space inside the walls where they had heard workers installing the dynamite. Somebody needed to sleep next to the walls. It was when the guards starting taking full advantage of this additional fear that things got out of hand. There were fist-fights over sleeping arrangements almost daily. Guards frequently exploded paper bags outside the walls in the night, causing panic attacks and screams and nightmares.

As was usually the case, the population came to Mateo and his advisory council, as it came to be known, to find a solution.

One of the things that was missing in the prison barracks was a sense of time. There were no clocks, and of course no radio to announce the hour. There was no regularity with regard to meal-time, or a specific hour when the prisoners were marched out to the gardens to work. At first some of the council members chuckled at Mateo when he suggested specific times to meet regarding the particular issues to be discussed. They would wander over to the meeting area when they thought it was approximate, but with no sense of urgency. When Mateo chastised one of them in front of the others for his tardiness, they finally had to ask him how he knew whether they were late or early. Some were incredulous to his claim that he knew to the minute what the time of day or night was. Friendly bets were placed, and the entire population soon heard about the claim. Someone who had a better relationship with one of the guards who had a watch convinced him to confirm Mateo's claim to fame.

For Mateo, it wasn't a matter of proving anything. Whether people believed him or not made no difference to him. He knew his internal clock batteries hadn't diminished. For him, it was just the same as his heart-beat. He didn't consciously keep his heart beating day in and day out, and he didn't make a decision to keep his internal clock running, either. It had just become as much a part of him as the birthmark under his left armpit.

He was surprised at the fervor of the men when the guard finally came around to give him his big test. There was definitely a serious shortage of entertainment for them, if this was going to be the highlight of their day.

With his fancy watch in his hand, Pareta, the guard who had just recently dropped a big chunk of ice outside the fence, laughing while it melted in front of the eyes of a dozen prisoners, called Mateo over to the fence. "When I give you the signal, you tell me what time you think it is."

There was a silence in the yard like never before, as the group watched Pareta's arm poised in the air like a conductor preparing for the first note in a symphony. For the benefit of the group, he turned the face of his watch so that some of the prisoners could see it, but it was out of Mateo's sight line. He brought his arm down and pointed to Mateo. "What time is it, now?"

"It's exactly 11;28, and twenty seconds." There was a murmur from the group who could see the watch. Close, but not correct.

"Guess you need a new set of batteries, Mateo," chuckled the guard. "You're more than two minutes off the mark."

"Do you set your watch monthly or weekly with Radio Reloj?" was Mateo's quiet response.

There was a pause. "I set it on the first of every month, at six o'clock in the morning."

"Today's the 26th, and I'm guessing you need to set your watch forward a bit every month..., like maybe, two and a half minutes."

The guard laughed him off, strapping his shiny silver watch back onto his wrist, and turning on his polished military-issue boots.

Mateo smiled and turned back to the issue of the day. "There'll be a meeting of the council today at two p.m. Give or take two minutes." The group cracked up and Mateo laughed with them.

Before the group had completely disbursed, Pareta came out of the guard office, waving at the group. He had his watch in his hand again, and a little transistor radio in the other, tuned to Radio Reloj, the twenty-four-hour-a-day countdown of the hours and minutes.

"Two minutes and fifteen seconds!" Pareta shouted over the crowd noise.

That brought the group to a halt.

Pareta approached the fence again, a look of disbelief on his face he was unable to conceal even after years of being a prison guard. He motioned for the guys to approach the fence – the ones who'd been looking at his watch earlier. "Tell Mateo there'll be ice in the water at chow tonight." He turned and walked back toward the guard shack, still shaking his head. A cold drink of water would be like Christmas for everyone there. Mateo's legendary status just climbed another rung on the ladder.

The problem with the explosives in the walls hadn't been resolved, though, and that was the first priority for Mateo. The nervous tension it caused was literally a ticking time bomb in the barracks. Somebody was going to snap, and soon. The council met and argued about how to convince the guards to get rid of the explosives. Most of the council shared the same opinion, and it revolved around begging or demanding the guards to remove the explosives. Unfortunately, they all knew those methods hadn't proven fruitful over the past weeks and months, and even though there had been no accidental ignition of any of the dynamite, many were afraid that anything might set them off – even a stray dog or another animal that bumped against the wall at the wrong spot.

It was only when one of the other prisoners threatened to throw himself at the wall in a suicide mission that Mateo came up with his idea for a solution. Even though he was too far from home to have any visitors, there were a few men inside who had regular family visits. They lived near enough to travel to the prison weekly or biweekly. Mateo gave their "visitees" instructions. It wouldn't happen overnight, but the council agreed the idea was the best so far.

Each of the guards would be followed home, and their neighbors would be grilled for the names and ages of each of their children, where they went to school, what parks they played in, etc. When that information was brought back to the prison, the next phase of the project began.

At first it was almost unnoticeable; children's names were dropped subtly into conversations as the guards walked past. They wouldn't have even registered that someone had mentioned his child's name, but by the third or fourth time they heard a prisoner say the same name, and throwing in his age, and later the school name, and the teacher's name, and then the color of his lunchbox – bells began to go off. When the guards gathered and shared similar stories, the plan started to gain more ground.

Every child has a weakness, and most share a weakness for a cool ice cream treat on a hot day. A few days after the name-dropping had sunk in, free ice cream cones were handed out to certain kids after school – all of them happened to be children of prison guards. Some of those kids might have spilled a little chocolate on their school uniforms, and others might have casually mentioned at the dinner table that they'd been given free ice cream by a nice lady after school.

Another session of prisoners bringing up their children's names as they made their rounds near the fence after the ice cream gifts, and there would be another level of nerves with the guards.

By the third week, Mateo felt like it was time for the knock-out punch, and had the final instructions delivered to the visiting wife of one of the prisoners. A giant dart board was drawn, and on it were the names of each of the guards' children. Below the dart board was a simple message: "Time to remove the explosives." It was delivered to the guard shack by a little girl, with a cake covered with sparklers that had been lit just before she knocked on the door.

The message was received, loud and clear. The work crews came in the same afternoon and removed the explosives from the prison walls. Most of the guards had already requested and were granted transfers for their entire families.

Terrorism was a double-edged sword, they learned.

Mateo's value as a prisoner was growing more and more every day, and it wasn't lost on the prison guards that things had changed radically in the short time since he had been transferred into a general population. They realized, maybe a little too late, that Mateo was someone they were better off keeping isolated. And especially with the official visit from Sergeant Pomares coming up so soon.

The fifth anniversary of the triumph of the revolution was approaching in December, and soon after it came the fifth anniversary of Mateo's imprisonment for collaboration with the Batista forces. No one knew better than Mateo how long it had been since he had tasted freedom, or seen his girlfriend, or his mother and sisters. Time was his friend at times, but a bitter enemy at others. The seconds and minutes and hours ticked inside his head, like it or not, reminding him constantly of how his future was slipping away. He could only push the thoughts of his mother and wife and sisters from his head for limited amounts of time in each day, but they forced their way in each time he let down his guard. It was hardest when the wind blew from the direction of the kitchen of the guard house, and the odor of some ingredient would assault his senses – usually onion or garlic, the staples of a Cuban kitchen. It was always something they were preparing for themselves – never the tasteless, unsalted mash for the prisoners. Mateo's subconscious mind would transport him to the front porch of his house in Topes de Collantes, where he would usually find one or the other of the women of the house peeling garlic or picking the little stones out of the rice to prepare the mid-day meal. He would often be carrying the morning's eggs, or maybe a freshly-plucked chicken for the pot. His mother, bless her soul, could make a man cry with the flavor she could wring out of a chicken. She knew when to sprinkle the cumin, and how to massage the onion and garlic mixture into the skin, and how to use just the amount of tomato sauce, made from her own grandmother's recipe. From thy bounty...

Luckily for Mateo, no one ever gave him time to let melancholy sink in very deep. There was always a question from someone who needed his wisdom or advice. Even if it was just the best way to trap mice to add a little substance to the rice water, as they called it.

One of the guards who didn't know anything about Mateo's history, let it slip that they were preparing for a royal visit from Sergeant Pomares, which was the reason for the extra detail in the yard clean-up and even a fresh coat of paint, mostly to hide the patches where the explosives had been removed. Mateo fell into a silence that began to frighten those nearest him in the pecking order. He even wandered in late for one of their council meetings, which had never happened in the past.

Mateo hated the idea of sharing the same air with the man who had taken away everything he ever had. On the other hand, he couldn't give the bastard the satisfaction of thinking he had broken his old neighbor and nemesis.

As the day of the visit came closer, Mateo asked some favors of the council and the families of the frequent visitors. Because of the scarcity of soap and water and even the dullest of razor blades, almost all of the prisoners had left their beards to grow and their uniforms were every color other than their original. There were a few barbers in the group, so Mateo had them work in shifts with the one pair of scissors and half dozen razors they were able to get in with the laundry soap they had arranged for. The dirt floor began to look like a carpet as beards and hair covered a dozen square meters of the corner furthest from the scrutiny of the guards. Those who knew how to wash clothes kept busy scrubbing the filth with the limited amount of water they could find.

By the morning of Pomares' arrival, the men looked downright civilized. The guards did a double take when they saw the clean faces and clothes on the prisoners. Trying to find the scissors and razor blades would mean hours of digging and searching that they didn't have. There was plenty more to do before the visit.

Only a select group knew of Mateo's relationship with Pomares, and they were not sharing it with the rest of the men. They had discussed it, out of his earshot, vowing to ensure things didn't get out of hand if they ended up face to face.

The Lada Nivas came down the long palm-lined lane to the prison area, all shined and polished for the occasion. The first and last ones sported little Cuban flags fastened to the radio aerials. When the press van showed up a few minutes after the Nivas, the prison staff realized there was much more to this visit than the regular inspection they had been advised. Nerves were on edge as the pitchers of ice water and coffee were prepared for the dignitaries. One tiny cup was dropped, splashing coffee onto the director's clean and pressed slacks. He shot a look of fire at the young orderly who had dropped it, but there was no time to do anything about it. The little handle of the cup had been broken off, rendering it useless for an official visit – it would serve perfectly well for every other day of the year, but not this day. With no extra cups, someone would need to refuse the traditional greeting of sweet espresso. The director made a silent signal to his second in command. He would make an excuse of blood pressure, or something, prohibiting him from the coffee.

The orderly hurried back to make another pot of coffee for the press, trying to count the heads in the van, and searching for enough broken cups for them. Press wasn't the same as the upper brass.

Since the Nivas were two door models, there was no dignified manner of dismounting from the rear seat. Sergeant Pomares rode shotgun in the final vehicle, but each of the others waited until he was at the front of the line before exiting theirs. Most of them had been on the receiving end of one of his rants about decorum with respect to rank. There'd been demotions and deductions in pay or vacation days for tiny infractions that the Sergeant felt slighted him in the least. When he reached the steps to the main office, he nodded for the others to join him, and motioned to the person attending the front door that he could summon the director.

The tripods were being arranged around the steps that led to the small covered deck area next to the entrance to the office. Somebody found a podium from where Sergeant Pomares could make his short speech. There were only half a dozen staff members in the office – the guards were all positioned around the barracks and in their stations, looking extremely attentive and being careful not to wrinkle their freshly-laundered uniforms. One of them tried not to think about the rash on his neck from the starched collar he was unaccustomed to buttoning to the top.

Sergeant Pomares signaled to the director that it was time to provide his introduction to the small gathering of press, and there was a heartfelt, if not obligatory, show of hands by the entourage, followed immediately by the members of the press, who realized they should clap for the sergeant, even before he had said a word.

His speech could have been written from memory by any of the press gallery: it was the typical rehashing of every speech given by every Communist Party member – things were so much better in the new Revolutionary Cuba, led by their beloved and respected Commandant Castro and guided by the far-seeing and ever-diligent Che Guevara. The bourgeois landowners and Yankee business interests had been ousted righteously, and Pomares stretched his arm and motioned to the prison yards where the filth that wanted nothing but to bring back the injustice were being taken care of and fed, with their families provided for in decent housing provided by the State. He spouted the statistics of the number of schools that had been, or were being built, the hospitals and clinics sprouting from every community in every province. The literacy programs were in full swing, leaving no Cuban without knowing how to read and write, because knowledge was the real power. Ideas would be the future fortune of Cuba under the glorious Revolution.

The press nodded their heads and stopped writing to clap when they saw the soldiers do so, and dutifully wrote everything down, even though it would be edited by others before it could be printed, just in case there was a poor choice of words that didn't provide the correct luminescence to the Revolution. One of the soldiers who had been driving all night to attend the ceremony, slipped out of attention during a pause in the speech, and caught the sharp eyes of Sergeant Pomares, who needed no help from a written speech to spout his well-practiced jargon. He saw the flicker of Pomares' gaze fall to his chest, where his last name and badge number were, and he felt the jolt of cold sweat that told him he would be looking for work elsewhere the following day.

In the barracks, several hundred men in their cleanest clothes, some the uniform of the prison, some their own street clothes, listened to the speech that was projected over a poor quality loud speaker. It wasn't clear, but they knew the jist of it. They were to feel privileged that Fidel and his benevolent Party members had chosen to provide them with such generous conditions, instead of slaughtering them like dogs and leaving their families to starve.

Mateo's mind was in his coffee-groves, smelling the ripe beans and feeling the cool dampness of Topes de Collantes. He could do this when it was necessary. Being so close to the only person in the world he actually hated made it his only method of maintaining his dignity. He felt his fists clench and unclench involuntarily. He turned on his internal clock and counted the seconds and minutes of the speech, while subconsciously tightening the cinch of his horse to compensate for the weight of the coffee it carried in the woven sacks.

Twelve minutes, thirty-five seconds. His eyes snapped open when he heard the roar of praise and exaggerated clapping from the captive audience. There was no clapping from inside the barracks – only a collective series of expletives and sounds of disgust.

Pomares and the director withdrew into the comfort of the main office, while the press crew packed their gear to head for the next speech from the next Revolutionary spokesperson. The soldiers were allowed to stand at ease, but not to seek any refuge from the hot sun. One pulled out a cigarette, and was about to strike a match to it when he heard the clearing of a superior's throat.

Mateo felt a need to be alone; far too many of the prisoners knew either first- or second-hand of his history with Pomares – maybe not all of the details – none of them knew about Mateo's nephew Juanito, and no one would ever learn that detail from him. He ignored the visual invitations from several of the leadership group, and made his way to the furthest corner of the building, close to the makeshift bathrooms. It was disgusting there, but

Mateo could push the stink away in his mind, and the solitude was worth the price for him at any rate.

He forced himself into his exercise of picturing his mother and sisters, and even tried to age little Juanito in his mind. For some reason, he was having trouble seeing Gladys' image lately. He knew in his heart she wouldn't have waited for him. They had never even consummated their marriage, anyway, so who could really blame her? He'd heard from another prisoner from Topes a few years later that she and her mother had taken her father's death very badly, and had gone to live with family near Santiago de Cuba. He hoped she was happy there, and had moved on with her life.

More than half an hour had passed since Pomares had entered the guard house, and Mateo was deep in his own mind, so he didn't hear the murmurs and activity surrounding the opening of the main gates to the barracks, and the swarm of camouflage around the Sergeant, who had suggested an unscheduled inspection of the barracks. The director feigned delight at the idea, while his panic-stricken eyes urged the other guards to action. This was the first time since the camp had opened that an official officer would set foot inside the gates that separated the prisoners from their sworn enemy. He had a knot forming between his shoulder blades, where his tension centered itself as he did his best to channel his primary school acting talent, planting a smile on his face that said he was delighted by the idea to show off his little slice of paradise.

It was a tie as to which group was most surprised when the main doors opened and Sergeant Pomares and the director came face to face with a wall of clean-shaven, bathed men in civilized clothing, almost all with their shirts tucked in and buttons done up high on their chests. The director did an about face – he had never seen anything but filth and unkempt beards and foul odors that made it difficult to not cover his mouth with the clean white handkerchief his wife always ironed and folded neatly and left beside his breakfast plate each morning. He unconsciously straightened up and lifted his chin off of his collar. He had dreaded the idea that the sergeant would want to personally inspect the conditions, and knew the prisoners would like nothing more than to make him look as negligent as humanly possible. He silently wondered what had gotten into them as he painted a smile on his face for the sergeant and followed him deeper within the enemy territory. He was thankful for the dozen armed guards standing at attention next to the train of Lada Nivas not more than fifty meters from the gate to the barracks.

Sergeant Pomares had added an extra inch of lift to his boots, trying to overcome a complex over his lack of height. He had also commissioned a seamstress to add a layer of extra mass to his chest, making him look more muscular than he really was. A simple threat of prison for her son had kept her silent. Power had its privileges. He strutted around the facility, seeming to enjoy the fact he had been responsible for so much of it. He had personally consulted with Che and el Commandante Fidel to set the guidelines by which these bourgeois landowners and thieves would be sentenced, leaving their trappings to be justly redistributed for the good of the country, (and a small percentage set aside for his own benefit at a later date). He had requisitioned the chicken farm this had once been to be reinforced and made into the high volume prison facility it was. One of his freezers still held several dozen of the chickens they had "redistributed".

He paused to watch one of the little curly-tailed lizards as it scampered between the blocks of the nearest barrack. He was almost surprised it hadn't been trapped and eaten yet. Trying to make it look as though his tour through the facility was random, he detoured to walk through the rows of the garden area, even stopping to inspect a stalk of corn.

Mateo needed to be as far away as possible from the person he most hated in life – actually the ONLY person he could honestly say he hated. He glanced up at the sun, as if to use it to judge the time of day, when he knew the time to the second with his eyes closed on the cloudiest day. Sometimes, like at this moment, the ticking of his internal clock deafened him. His only defense was to find a place to be alone, and to force his mind back to before all of this. Back to his horse – the smell of the straw in his stall, the crunch the oats as it munched contentedly, swishing the flies away with the flick of its tail. And that crazy multi-colored cat, showing up at any time, pouncing at him from the most impossible places.

Something forced Mateo out of his memory. It couldn't have been any of the inmates, because they knew not to approach him when he was out at the far corner of the complex. There was so little privacy in the prison, so it became a sacred thing to everyone. If someone was at the corner of the fence, where the branch of the banyan tree a dozen yards outside provided a rare stain of shade, nobody encroached on them. They all knew that everyone needed a little time on their own, and especially Mateo. He spent day and night counseling the others – mostly the new guys, helping them to settle in and find the routines that were so important to survival.

At the sound of approaching boots on the worn trail, Mateo opened his eyes and turned to face the guards. He knew it couldn't be inmates because none of them had boots solid enough to crack the gravel as they approached, and they didn't walk in time to some inner beat. He was unpleasantly surprised to see that the person leading the small group was Sergeant Pomares. Mateo swallowed hard, putting on his unemotional mask, stood up to his full height, and unconsciously straightened the wrinkles of his whitest shirt. He wondered what new idea Pomares had dreamed up to break him, this time. At least he was going to do it to his face, unlike the previous attempts.

"I see you're adapting to your new home," Pomares began, stopping a few yards from where Mateo stood. "I assume the shaved faces and clean shirts was your idea."

"Human dignity is something that existed a long time before I came along." Mateo maintained his tone as unemotional as possible.

"We have different ideas of what dignified looks like, I suppose." Pomares felt the familiar tingle of power over his nemesis. "How is your foot?" He liked to remind Mateo of who was responsible for his permanent limp.

"As long as I don't need to count higher than 18, everything is fine."

The guard who stood beside the prison warden chuckled at the comment, and was immediately stifled by a stern look from his boss.

"I wanted to give you the news personally, so I arranged this inspection."

Mateo's eyes darted to Pomares'. News? What news would the sergeant possibly want to give him personally? Another move? Further away, still?

Pomares turned to the prison warden, who handed him a folder, from which he pulled two official-looking papers. With some hesitation, he read the words from the first: it was full of legal jargon and justification, but the gist of the message was that Mateo's sentence had been served. Today was to be his final day in prison, provided he signed the papers promising no legal or other retaliation for his incarceration.

Mateo was numb. He could feel his blood coursing through his veins, pounding his temples. Was he hearing correctly? He had never even had a trial. No one had ever told him how long he was supposed to be in prison. He had come to assume it was until he died, or Fidel died, or Pomares died.

While he pondered the hundred things assaulting his brain, Pomares held his hand up, signaling there was more. "I assume you have had no contact from your family." Mateo nodded affirmatively. "Then I will give you this news as a former neighbor, and not a military official. This other paper, unfortunately, is a copy of the death certificate for your mother.

Mateo stared at Pomares like he was trying to figure out what planet he was from. What was he saying? His mother couldn't be dead. She was waiting for him to get out so they could go back to their farm and get on with life with his sisters and nephew. She couldn't be dead, because no one had ever told him she was even sick.

"What?" The only things that could come out of his head were monosyllabic. "When? Where? How?" He went through the basic questions, not waiting for an answer to any of them, and stopping short before asking the only question to which he already knew the answer – 'why'.

Pomares handed the two papers to one of the guards, and signaled for him to give them to Mateo, who could no longer hold his legs under him, and he tossed the clemency letter to the side and clutched the certificate like it was his mother's skirt. His face was distorted into a living version of the scream painting. Only no scream came out of his mouth. He studied the paper, as though by staring at it he could erase the words on it – the name, date of birth, and finally the date of death. He paused, reading it over and over, trying to make it register on his brain that seemed to have abandoned him suddenly. She had died nearly six months earlier! His unconscious mind started calculating against his will – 140 days... 3360 hours... 201,600 seconds... that his mother had been dead, and he didn't know it. How long had she been sick? How long had she waited for him to come to her assistance?

"Where is she now, at this moment?" His voice came back to him suddenly, and he was frantic to get to his mother. He looked at the other paper on the ground a few feet away. He reached for it, held it toward Pomares. "This says I can leave. I want to leave now... right now."

"Your family has been relocated to Pinar del Rio. I can make arrangements for you to be taken there if you wish. You will just need to sign the papers that the warden has prepared in his office." Pomares made a big performance of pulling his pocket watch out, flipping open the cover so that it was exposed clearly to Mateo, and then replacing it slowly and methodically.

There was a desperation in Mateo that was uncharacteristic, and his fists clenched and unclenched involuntarily, crumbling the papers into two balls.

"We have the paperwork for you to sign at the office. There are fourteen people who will leave today." Pomares signaled for two of the chaperones to help Mateo to his feet, but he shrugged them off.

"I'd like to say good-bye to the men."

Pomares assumed his full stature, rigid and assuming. "I'm afraid that's not possible. We find it upsets the men, so we prefer to make it quick and quiet. The warden has already taken the others through a back exit. We're just waiting for you, now."

Mateo flashed back over the years he'd spent in prison – friends he'd made and friends he'd lost. He hated the idea of abandoning the others without saying good-bye, but he had a much more powerful sentiment that told him to run, not walk, to the gate, before he woke up and found this to be another of his recurring dreams of freedom. He needed to get to his sisters, and to ensure that his mother had been properly taken care of.

"How can I get to my family?" Mateo's face had changed to almost statuesque – no more emotion – only resolve. His voice was monotone. No emotion whatsoever. His eyes turned to Pomares. "Get me out of this place, then."

"One of the Jeeps will take you and two of the others to the compound in Pinar del Rio where your families have been living. There are people there to make arrangements for your future."

Mateo wasn't listening anymore. He focused his entire being on his next move, which was to get to his sisters. His mind snapped the hour into his head – four fifteen and twenty seconds. He started to calculate the distance from Pinar del Rio and how many hours before he would be with his sisters. He didn't know the route they would take, or the condition of the roads or the speed of the Jeep, but he knew every minute he wasn't moving in their direction was lost, and he motioned to the guards to get moving, and made sure he didn't look behind him, for fear he'd see the faces of his companions who weren't leaving. Focus. Fence. Office. Papers. Jeep. Family.

PART EIGHT

It was nearly two hours before the last paper was signed, and the final prisoner had received his personal effects. Mateo wasn't surprised to learn that his things had been lost in the transfer to the other location. There was nothing that would have fit him anyway from ten years earlier. Ten years, three months, eleven days, and now eighteen hours, fifteen minutes, since they'd thrown him and his father-in-law-to-be into the hole outside of Topes de Collantes, where he'd spent his youth. He came in a young man, and was leaving a middle-aged shell of his former self. He was conscious of the fact that he no longer stood up to his full six feet plus. He had a permanent bend from years of sleeping on beds shorter than his body.

Bent, maybe, but not broken.

The sound of the Jeep's engine cranking to life was like a symphony to Mateo, and he released an audible sigh as it jumped into motion. He'd never learned to drive anything more than a small tractor, but he knew the concept, and he subconsciously went through the motions with the driver as he shifted through the four gears and started the journey he'd been thinking about every waking hour since he'd been imprisoned.

The sun was already low in the western sky, and the shadows from the sparse trees along the road caused them to alternate between light and dark frequently. Finally, after less than an hour on the road, there was no longer any sunlight, and the Jeep's headlights were their only guide. Mateo noticed that the passenger side lamp was loose, and poorly adjusted, providing as much light to the ditch along the road as it did to the poorly-maintained highway. It danced with every little bump in the road, and there were plenty of them. A particularly deep rut the driver couldn't avoid jarred them out of their seats and Mateo felt his hair brush the canvas of the Jeep's top. He was reminded of the day so long ago when he'd seen Che Guevara pass by him. He thought about the deep burn scars he still carried with him on his chest as a reminder, and of how he'd made the joke that he'd shared a cigar with Che. He remembered the look on Pomares' face as he'd aimed his rifle at him, and the pain when he'd lost his toes from the bullet.

Choices he'd made, and the consequences that followed.

They passed a coffee plantation and Mateo's eyes welled up with emotion. He tried to focus on the flock of parrots he saw flying nearby, but they swooped low over a pair of harnessed horses munching on some green grass near the barbed-wire fence, and his past life started to haunt him.

He made himself listen to the conversation of his companions in the back seat of the Jeep, pulling his thoughts back to the present. Mateo the farm boy had perished long ago. He looked at his hands – cracked and scarred from neglect and poor diet, his once-powerful wrists and arms that could pull his weight up on his hand-made chin bar beside the roasting shack looked like those of a much older man – discolored from years of over-exposure to a relentless sun, covered in spots from lack of vitamins in the prison meals. What would these hands be good for now? he wondered to himself, as the Jeep rounded a long bend and the dancing headlight surprised a fox that had planned to cross the highway, and stared into the light, frozen in time. Its eyes looked almost fluorescent, reflecting the Jeep's light back at them. Just in time it changed its course and avoided being a meal for the vultures that were never far away.

Mateo tried to strike up a conversation with the driver, but found he didn't remember how to have a normal conversation. The weather, the quality of the mangos and avocados this year, where he was from, and Mateo realized he was out of topics, because everything else could be taken as political, and he knew that was dangerous territory. The driver must have been instructed to only speak when spoken to, because his mono-syllabic responses and absence of eye contact were obvious indicators that he wasn't interested in small talk.

One of the guys in the back seat took the initiative to strike up a medley of old familiar tunes. He had a reasonable singing voice, and soon had his buddy joining in on the choruses. Mateo found himself tapping his toes – what was left of them, anyway – along with the melodies. He hadn't heard anyone singing out of joyfulness since his mother, before his father had died.

The jolt to his heart to even think about his mother yanked him back from the momentary feeling of that thing called happiness he had almost forgotten existed. His mind invented the final moments of her life, his sisters doing their best to comfort her, but he knew she would have died waiting to see him again. He brushed his dry arm across his eyes. Better not to think about it. Maybe he could sleep and wake up in his sisters' arms. He closed his eyes and leaned his head against the arm that held the handle above the opening where the door might have been had there been one. There were too many curves and too many bumps in the pavement, though, and he fell into his old faithful habit of counting. There were concrete power poles along the side of the highway, and he counted the seconds between them, keeping track of the variation in speed of the Jeep due to curves and road conditions. An average of thirteen seconds between them when he had counted a hundred times. He started to calculate the distance based on the speed of the Jeep, if the speedometer was correct at approximately eighty-five kilometers an hour. He saw a sign that announced la Habana to be one hundred and ten kilometers ahead, and he figured out the approximate time of arrival. He had never been even close to the capital city in his life, so it gave him something to look forward to. He had a mission, now. How many power poles until Havana? If there were thirteen seconds between them at eighty-five kilometers an hour, then there would be approximately six poles for every mile, or three and a half per kilometer, so that meant there would be about three hundred and eighty five poles between him and la Habana. He wished he could convince the driver to speed up to a hundred kilometers an hour, just to make the math easier, and of course to get there sooner. Three hundred and eighty four. Three hundred and eighty three. He could handle this.

Unfortunately for Mateo, they wouldn't see much of Havana, as the highway skirted the city when they finally arrived, three hundred and sixty-six poles later. His math had been out by some decimal points, thankfully in his favor. Still, though, he could now say he'd been to the capital of his country, or at least the place that once had been his country. The first thing he noticed as they turned onto the multi-lane street that would take them past the international airport was the number of vehicles on the road, and the wide streets with three and sometimes four lanes each way. The next thing he noticed were all of the revolutionary billboards, spewing slogans and propaganda as far as the eye could see. The city was beautiful, he could tell. There were parks and trees and sculptures and construction everywhere. He could see giant steel cranes towering above the skyline. Approaching the turn toward the airport, he saw a gigantic airplane making its final approach, looking like it was going to land right on them. It was deafening as it passed over their heads, and Mateo could clearly see the Russian hammer and sickle painted on the side of it. As he assimilated the idea of a Russian transport plane landing in his capital, he began to notice the heavy military presence on nearly every corner, with serious-looking young soldiers carrying heavy rifles. Military green seemed to be the prominent color of vehicles on the street, and most looked Russian in style, or lack there-of.

There was a clover-leaf overpass near the airport that Mateo had only seen in the old movies he'd attended in Trinidad as a kid. One of the exits indicated Pinar del Rio, and he could feel the nerves tighten. He couldn't wait to be on the highway to his sisters, and watched for any indication of the distance.

The guys in the back of the Jeep maintained a constant conversation between them, mostly talking about what meals they wanted first, and how many beers they would drink with them. There was lots of laughter from them, in stark contrast to the silence in the front. Mateo's calculating brain was estimating the arrival time based on their current speed – not measured by the Jeep's malfunctioning speedometer, but by the count between the kilometer markers on the side of the highway. Approximately forty-five seconds between each km, so they were travelling at about thirty-five miles per hour.

Aside from having an internal clock in his head, ticking off the hours, minutes and seconds of his life, Mateo had an enhanced sense of body language. He recognized when someone's jaw was set in a way that meant they were stressed about something, or when someone's palms were sweating out of context with the temperature. There were dozens of other "tells", but he had noticed the driver's jaw and palms had changed significantly since they had passed the cloverleaf. Added to that were the frequent glances in the rear-view mirror, indicating he was watching for something or someone. There was no mirror on the passenger side, so Mateo made a point of shifting in his seat to make a comment to the other two passengers, but it was really to allow his peripheral vision out the glass-less rear window. The Jeep was obviously capable of significantly higher speeds, and the driver's nervousness was beginning to set off alarms in Mateo's head. These alarms had saved his life on more than one occasion, so he paid close attention.

When he saw what the driver had obviously been watching for, he felt the slight reduction in speed, and the change in camber of the engine. Approaching fast were three heavier military vehicles, similar to the trucks that had carried Pomares more than ten years earlier when he'd lost his toes. His mind went into survival mode, and he scanned the terrain around them, looking for escape routes.

They were never going to be taken to their families. They were just to be removed from the prison and made to disappear quietly. Some lie would be prepared to cover up their unfortunate "accident", and things would go back to normal again. There was an overpass approaching, spanning what looked to be some kind of river or stream. Mateo couldn't make out what it was from half a kilometer away, but with no other cover on either side of the highway, he decided it was his best hope. He knew the two guys in the back seat wouldn't be able to get out with him, but he did his best with his eyes to let them know that they needed to do something, too, because the convoy of trucks wasn't there to give them a hero's escort. He was lucky to be in the front, with no door to impede his exit, just the idea of hitting the shoulder of the road at more than thirty miles an hour. Hit the ground rolling, he told himself. If he couldn't get up and run, he wouldn't have time to worry about how much it hurt.

Mateo turned himself back to face the front of the Jeep, and did his best to look like he was relaxing for the rest of the journey, stretching his right leg outside of the vehicle, and finding purchase on the welded step. He calculated where he'd need to grab the windshield post in order to throw himself clear of the rear wheel. One of the two in the back seat was doing his own calculations; how quickly he could choke the driver from behind. They were still a hundred meters from the overpass when Mateo saw him go for it, and he knew this was his chance. As the arm sprung around the driver's neck like a bear trap, unfortunately instead of braking, his foot pressed the throttle to the floor, jerking the Jeep into a steep acceleration. It made the force necessary to throw himself clear threefold, but Mateo knew he had to make his move, and grabbed the window post with his left hand, the back of the seat with his right, and launched himself. He could see the driver's hands leave the wheel to grasp at the strong grip from behind, and as he felt the first jagged stones tear into his flesh, the first round of machine-gun fire rang out from very close behind.

In his mind, while visualizing the event, Mateo had seen himself rolling along the ground like a long, narrow barrel, maybe half a dozen times, then coming to a stop. The reality was much different – instead of a barrel, his body was flailing around like an out-of-round tire, his shoulders hitting the ground, then his rear end, then his feet, then his opposite shoulder, his other hip, a knee that had flown out of line, then the back of his head took the brunt of the next round, and instead of slowing down gracefully, he felt like he was actually gaining speed and losing form. Now he was a triangle, bouncing head-rump-heels; now a parallelogram, with an arm forming part of the shape. He had no time to think about anything specific, except when this ride would end. He knew there must be bones broken somewhere, but bullets flying past him took precedence over bones. There was some law of gravitational pull or inertia that he remembered that said a body in motion would climb towards a fulcrum, or a crown, or some such thing. He'd made the belt on the old feed chopper stay on the flat pulley by winding tape around the middle of it. So he understood the concept, and understood why he was actually climbing up the ditch toward the highway instead of descending to the lowest point. The problem was that the highway was soon to give way to a concrete bridge, and there didn't seem to be much give to the concrete that he saw coming at him with each consecutive vault. Bullets or bridges would have the same effect.

The pain stabbed him deeply when he thrust his left arm out of the human ball he had tried to make of himself, not very effectively, to be sure. He was sure his arm disconnected itself from his shoulder, but his next flip showed him that he had indeed changed course and would miss the concrete of the bridge narrowly. The only problem now was the next view he had was a whole lot of nothing. In the instant that he passed the two-foot-thick column, he saw the almost vertical drop down toward water. Not very deep water, either. His only salvation was the thick brush and small trees that had grown up along the banks of the creek or river, whatever it was – and he could feel his velocity diminishing quickly. Mateo gasped at the pain from a limb breaking under his weight, a sharp broken branch leaving another gouge in the flesh of his lower back. He was definitely slowing down, though, and could almost control himself by now. With his right arm and hand, he grasped at anything that came within reach, and finally got a hold of some thick brush that allowed him to swing himself around it and come to a stop. Pain. Lots of pain. Pain was good, though, he told himself, because if he was dead he wouldn't feel any pain. He must REALLY be alive, then, he thought to himself, in the split second between coming to a stop, and knowing that stopped was the opposite of what would keep him alive. He managed a quick glance up the steep slope, to see if he could see anyone coming toward him, and at that moment he heard the distinctive shouts for mercy from his two companions, and then not two, but three bursts of gunfire. The driver had been forcibly retired from his post, he surmised. He knew they'd be after him now that the others had been taken care of, so pain or no pain, he turned back to the task of descending to the thicker brush and find a place to hide. Taking inventory of his body parts, he decided he had one working arm, one knee that could bend, and could flex the foot with the three and a half toes. Not bad, considering. He was thankful that gravity was on his side, as he mostly just slid downward, doing his best to avoid anything sharp. He set his sights on the thickest brush that was closest to the water. It was also downstream from the bridge, which might give him a chance to swim if the water was deeper there. He heard a lot of chatter from above, but couldn't make anything out. Somebody was going to be in big trouble if they didn't get their prime target.

He pushed his way as deep into the thicket as he could, trying to bend, not break, the branches, and inwardly growling to himself every time he grasped a sharp thorn. He was deep enough in that it was dark when he heard the curses of one of the attackers trying to control his descent down the slope. He lost the battle, halfway down, and rained a string of fowl things that didn't end until Mateo heard the thud of his pursuer land a dozen yards from him. Mateo was thankful he couldn't see the other man, which meant he was probably just as invisible. There was a distinctive groan as the soldier tried to stand, and another shower of profanities that would have kept Mateo sleeping in the barn for a month had he been caught by his mother. Just the thought of his mother having passed without him there pushed much of Mateo's pain into a vault, and gave him another round of rage and will to survive, if only to avenge his family.

A shout from up top about them needing to clean up the bodies and get moving was answered by the injured soldier telling him there was no sign of Mateo, and to throw down a rope to get him out of where he was. They were running out of time, which was Mateo's salvation, for now, anyway. Apparently they didn't want anyone else to see the execution-style killings on the highway, especially when one of the victims wore the same color uniform as they did.

Mateo had to remain statue-like while three soldiers up top extracted their injured mate. He couldn't take a chance that one of them would hear a branch snap or even a startled bird fly out of the brush he was encased in. It seemed to take forever, and it gave him time to feel the different pain centers screaming at him from his interior.

The extraction complete, Mateo heard the entire conversation between the soldiers as they dragged and coerced their companion to the top of the river valley. He confirmed what he already knew to be true. Pomares was behind everything. He couldn't hold them any longer, so he needed an accident to keep them quiet. The soldiers didn't know which one of their targets had been missed in the operation, but apparently they weren't about to risk the wrath of their commander. They agreed to tell him the fourth guy had fallen over the bridge when they'd shot him, and it was too far down to get him.

Mateo was dead. No longer existed. Nullified.

PART NINE

At first it took a while to sink in. How could he survive in a dictatorship that controls every person from morning to night, if he didn't exist to them? He couldn't work, couldn't get medical attention, and couldn't use a bank. The long list of things he couldn't do was giving him a headache to go along with the other dozen areas of his body trying to get his attention. He heard the big trucks' gears grinding as they tried to get as far from the scene of the events as possible in the shortest amount of time. As the last one left his ear-shot, he felt his muscles relax and finally allowed himself to lie on his back and rest. He'd take inventory of his injuries after he slept for just a few minutes.

As it turned out, Mateo slept better as a nobody than he had in the past ten years as a political prisoner. Somehow, in the flurry of negative points he had been noting in his little booklet in his mind, thoughts of how being dead to the world might just be the most freeing thing that had ever happened to him. He drifted off to the idea that he was, for the first time in more years than he cared to count, no longer under the control of anyone else. He thought he smelled coffee and that was his last conscious thought before he slept for five hours on a bed of thorny brush and a dislocated shoulder.

A dry mouth and the need to relieve himself eventually pulled Mateo out of his dream-filled sleep. He knew he needed to get himself out of the valley somehow, but first he needed to get to the water. With his functioning hand and arm, he fashioned a crude but helpful crutch to keep some of the weight off of what he was sure was just a badly-sprained ankle and knee, thankfully on the same side. So the right half of his upper body was in good shape, and the left half of his lower body was only bruised and a few dried cuts. All in all, he was about half the man he was when he'd jumped out of the Jeep half a dozen hours ago. He counted himself lucky, especially considering his two friends. He closed his eyes hard and tried to swallow the lump in his throat that tried to choke him from within. How many more?

The water was cool and after the first few handfuls splashed onto his face, Mateo gave in to his temptation and threw himself into the deepest, clearest part he could see in the semi-darkness. Little pin-pricks of pain reacted to the water, as dried wounds opened again and the clear water turned slightly pink around him. He decided an inventory was at hand, and peeled off his shirt and shoes and pants. He didn't like the look of the ankle as he had to force the sock to expand beyond its limit to free his lower leg and foot. His ankle was at least three times the size of its counterpart, and the swelling travelled down his foot to his three toes, exaggerating the result of his sharing the cigar with Che so long ago. For years Mateo had carried a plastic comb in his rear pocket. It had lost half of its teeth over time, but he chose not to replace it. It reminded him of himself, and it always brought a smile to his and others' faces when he wiped it across his blond locks.

He looked up through the trees and brush to the base of the bridge, some thirty yards above him, and decided that he'd wait until morning light to work on the climb out.

This time he knew he wasn't imagining it. Coffee – being toasted, not far away. He saw the leaves on the tree being persuaded from the north to the south, so the coffee roaster was north of him. Tomorrow he'd try to have a cup of coffee. That was his goal, and it kept him focused long enough to fashion a small shelter of branches and leaves to sleep for the night.

Not quite as good as the smell of his coffee, he decided as he found the most comfortable uncomfortable position. He shoved the last handful of the plums he'd found on one of the trees nearby into his mouth and tried to spit the seeds to the water a few yards away. He felt the tears well up again as his thoughts turned again to his sisters and his late mother and the 'almost' wife he'd hardly known. All his life, he'd countered negative thoughts by doing calculations in his head, or exercising until his focus returned to something constructive, like teaching the guy up north how to roast coffee beans. He didn't feel up to push-ups or chin-ups in his current state, so he set his mind to calculating how many pieces he could divide Pomares' body into with his bare hands. He knew that was anything but constructive, but it seemed to diminish the pain more than other methods he'd been trying.

The following morning, at five-forty-two, to be exact, Mateo splashed water on his unshaven face and ate the last few ripe plums. Instead of trying to climb up the steep bank to the bridge, he chose to follow the bank until the climb was less imposing. He was glad the cattle he came across were docile, and that they'd been downstream from him, considering what they were doing in the shallow water. Cattle meant someone who looked after the cattle, so he knew he would soon come across some sort of civilization, and that meant he needed a plan. Starting with a name. One of the men who had died in the Jeep had been named Manuel, but they called him Manolo. The other's last name had been Rodriguez. Good as anything, he decided. He was

Manolo Rodriguez, and he was on his way to see relatives in Pinar del Rio. Where was he from? His father had come from Camaguey as a boy, and always told fond stories about the big old Colonial houses there. He was Manolo Rodriguez, on his way from Camaguey to Pinar del Rio to visit – some cousins from Trinidad who'd been relocated there. He looked down at himself and decided he must have gotten beaten by some pretty nasty folks. Took everything he had.

PART TEN

It didn't take long for Mateo to get a chance to practice his acting – over the next rise in the terrain he spotted a double row trail with a raised center of grass in the middle, leading his eyes to a thin stream of smoke in a clearing of trees with a row of palm trees planted in a square pattern. Coffee. The swelling had subsided somewhat overnight on his ankle, allowing him to almost plant his weight on it without cursing, and the smell of the roasted beans was more of a painkiller than anything else. Anyone who roasted coffee was a kindred spirit to Mateo – or Manolo.

The owner of the property was an ancient man by the name of Paolo, but in his older age it had become Paolito, and he had invited Mateo into his home before he'd even gotten the first lie out of his mouth – old style manners and hospitality. He had a chipped glass of very bad coffee in his hands before he found his way to the wooden chair with the cow-hide seat that was so worn it was shiny like porcelain. From the untidiness of the place, Mateo gathered quickly that this was the home of a bachelor, or a widower, as it turned out. Paolito was quick to apologize for his mess – his Josefina would never have allowed it to get this way. She'd been gone for fifteen years, by then, he explained, so thankfully hadn't seen what had happened to the Cuba they had known.

Paolito caught himself mid-phrase, suddenly conscious of the fact that this stranger could be one more of those bastard secret police that came around counting his cattle and chickens and pigs and how many damned coffee bushes he had. Mateo did his best to put him at ease, but there was still a sense of doubt that pervaded the conversation.

"You been roasting coffee long?" Mateo started a conversation that he hoped would put his new friend at ease.

"My son did the roasting, until…" He didn't offer to finish the sentence, and Mateo knew enough not to insist.

"I could take a look," Mateo offered. "I used to be pretty good at it, back in Camaguey."

"Never heard there was much coffee that part of the country." Paolito's narrow brown eyes searched Mateo's face for clues.

"I worked for an uncle up in Topes de Collantes," Mateo responded, trying to make his lies a little easier to control. "His daughters are the cousins I want to visit in Pinar del Rio."

Paolito figured he could put this stranger to the test right then and there, and pointed to the back door. "Out there's my roasting oven – why don't we just head over and see what's what?"

Mateo forgot about his ankle for a second, and almost fell to the floor when he stood up. He used the chair to steady himself, and felt it crack under his weight. Things needed some adjusting here, he decided.

Words couldn't have described the feeling of Mateo's hands caressing the unroasted beans. Feeling their texture, their weight, how they sifted through his fingers. His eyes were closed – it was a visceral thing – he lifted a handful to his nose, even popped one bean into his mouth. Every sense was tuned to coffee. These weren't his beans – no doubt about that, but they had plenty of promise. Where to start, though? Everything here was wrong. Starting with the fire pit. His mind looked at images of his operation – well, his father's operation, but Mateo had made it his own with so many subtle adjustments. He looked around the sparse area, looking for any tools and materials he could work with. He saw almost nothing. "If I had my tools, I could probably fix most of this," he stated, almost apologetic.

"Well, that's where I can help." The older man's face lit up, and he seemed to straighten somewhat. "I don't know much about coffee, but I was a mechanic at a sugar mill for forty-five years. If it's a tool, I've got it!" He summoned Mateo to an alcove in the little shop, where there was a long hardwood work table with two different sized vices attached to opposite corners. He fished into his deep pocket for a ring of keys, and found the two he was looking for by touch. He swung the double doors wide, and Mateo actually gasped. "I keep them all cleaned and oiled and ready to work. These are my babies."

"Do you mind if I actually use them?" Mateo wasn't sure he was being offered the use of the tools, or just a trip to the tool museum.

"If you can remember to put them back where they came from."

That wouldn't be difficult, Mateo mused. Each tool had its own special space, with its outline painted carefully in red. Every wrench was hung on a nail in order. There were tools he'd never seen before, and many that he recognized from the mechanic's shop in Topes.

Mateo spotted a starting point – the sorting table, and set about to make it a copy of the one where he had spent so much of his youth, watching his father, and then mimicking him, even the way he hummed while he sorted the beans by color and size. Paolito's table was smaller than Mateo's, but once he had it on the right angle, and had tightened the legs and cross-bars so that it was on solid footing, he scooped two hands full of beans onto the surface. It was like music to Mateo.

Paolito leaned against the door frame for a few minutes, like a proud father watching the son he had lost too long ago. The strong hands of Mateo caressed the beans, rather than push them around the sizing screens, as Paolo had always done. The crackle of the beans falling through the opening onto the metal surface below took on a rhythm, and when he heard this stranger begin to hum, he knew he was no one to be feared. Nobody who loved coffee this much could be bad.

The roasting oven was all wrong... even as he fell into his dream-like state that he always had when he sorted the beans, his subconscious mind had been disassembling and reconstructing the oven. It was too high and too narrow – the beans wouldn't find the right balance of temperature and air-flow the way it was. But he would need to re-use the same bricks from the existing oven. By the time he had finished sorting the pile of beans, and had run out of tunes to hum, he had a plan in place. He'd seen a good file in the tool chest earlier, and would ask Paolito's permission to use the bench vice to change the angles of the bricks so that they formed a lower and wider configuration. He already knew how to rearrange the grate for the charcoal under it to make the heat more uniform. He'd adjusted his own so many times over the years that he could already feel the heat and smell the beans roasting.

His ankle reminded him that he couldn't put his weight on it yet, when he tried to stand. Five minutes later, he had tied an old rag onto a shovel handle he'd found, and he had a reasonably comfortable crutch to get around more easily. He was about to search for Paolito when the older man appeared with a small tray with two chipped coffee cups that had long lost their finger holders.

Mateo cringed as he took his first sip. It had been so long since anyone had offered him a freshly-brewed coffee that his eyes filled with tears.

"That bad, is it?" Paolito said, apologetically.

"It's not that," Mateo recovered. "I was just thinking about my uncle in Topes."

He took a second, longer drink. He moved the coffee around his pallet, swishing it between his teeth. "Actually, it IS that bad. It's awful!"

Both men laughed, and Mateo leaned against the work bench.

Paolito relaxed into a leather chair that appeared to have been molded to his body over the years. "My wife always made the coffee. I never really learned." He looked off to the side and upward, as though apologizing to his late wife for it.

"Not to worry, Paolito," Mateo intervened in his nostalgia. "Allow me to change the oven, and in two days I'll make you coffee worth drinking."

"It's a deal. Change whatever you want here. As you can see, my methods haven't exactly been working."

"Do you have a good shovel?" asked Mateo.

"Sure, should I bring it in here?"

"No, it's for you. I want you to bury the rest of the coffee you roasted before the coffee police catch you."

Paolito laughed like he hadn't since before he'd lost his wife and only son. Mateo placed his powerful hand on the older man's shoulder, and the laughter subsided and the old man covered his eyes with his sleeve to hide the tears.

"Dinner's at seven," said Paolito, recovering himself and using both hands to help himself back to his feet. "Don't be late," he chided.

"Can you cook better than you make coffee?" Mateo joked.

"My wife made the coffee, but she never learned to make a proper piece of meat, bless her soul. And wash your hands."

"I left my shirt and tie at the cleaners, but I'll clean myself up if you have a bar of soap and a razor."

It was nearly six forty by Mateo's inner clock when he finished sweeping the brick dust from the shop floor. The last bricks had been tricky to place, acting as keystones to hold the entire oven solidly with the reduced height. He'd taken them to a rough part of the concrete floor and scraped them until they were like glass. He found a large wooden hammer used for wood carving, and tapped bricks into place until there was no light filtering through any of them. There were dozens of stains from his sweat on the terracotta bricks when he tapped the last one into place. He would have precious little time to enjoy his first real shower in more than ten years. He checked the light switch to confirm there would be light after dinner to come back to work. The bulb flickered, failed, and then recovered to provide the minimum necessary.

He reached for the crutch, and reluctantly left the roasting shed.

The tang of onion and garlic assaulted Mateo long before he reached the house. And he had almost forgotten the aroma of cumin. This time he heard Paolito humming. Having someone else to cook for had rejuvenated him, and Mateo hurried his pace, not wanting to disappoint his host. Chicken stew – fricase – a life-long favorite of Mateo, and a lifetime since he'd sat down to a real meal. He wondered how his stomach would react to fresh food. This was the smell he'd tried to conjure all those years while he swallowed food not meant for hogs. He had a lump in his throat and was thankful that Paolito motioned him to the bathroom the moment he entered.

There Mateo found a towel that was almost transparent, but clean, and a fresh bar of soap, probably saved by the late wife as a decoration. There was a straight razor and a brush to make lather. Five stars, Mateo thought to himself, and he pulled back the curtain to find a metal pail nearly full with still-steaming water. The lump in his throat turned into a full-fledged sob, as Mateo couldn't help remembering how his mother had always had hot water ready for him to bath before the evening meal. He pulled the towel to his face and let himself cry for too long. More than ten years of holding everything in, never showing weakness to his captors or his fellow prisoners seemed to erupt at this moment.

Paolito's eyes watered in the kitchen, as he couldn't help but hear in the small house. He clicked on his old faithful transistor radio to give Mateo some modicum of privacy. There was far more to this young man's story, he mused. When he wanted to tell it, he would, he surmised, and turned his attention to checking the two best plates and water glasses. Tonight he would even pull out the crocheted table cloth.

Mateo emerged at seven o'clock sharp, freshly-shaven, and had even used the razor to make some sense of his hair in the little time he had, and with the mirror so opaque he could scarcely see himself.

Paolito looked at the ancient grandfather clock, the only piece of furniture that appeared to have any value, and shook his head. "You're late," he chided.

"I'd prefer to think that your clock is two minutes fast," but I'll accept your home-court advantage.

"You don't have a watch. How could you possibly argue?" Paolito shot him a look.

"It's a long story," Mateo responded, running his hand through his freshly-trimmed hair, and hobbled to the table without his crutch. "Looks like you have this under control."

"I love the kitchen." Paolito smiled as he expertly applied just the right amount of oil and vinegar to the green tomatoes and sliced onions. He pinched salt between his finger and thumb, and sprinkled it over the salad like he was an orchestra conductor, announcing the final note of Beethoven's Fifth Symphony. "Sit down, and prepare to be amazed."

Mateo couldn't help lifting his plate to his face, taking in the aroma of fresh rice, three pieces of a chicken that had been rooting in the yard only three hours earlier, and two of the tiny bananas that tasted like candy. The tomato sauce was exactly the right texture, with enough garlic and onion and cumin to cause his glands to reactivate in his throat. He almost didn't know when or where to start.

"Are you afraid it will burn you?" joked Paolito.

Mateo smiled and wiped his eyes. "It's been so long since I've eaten anything hot, I don't know how."

"Pick up a drumstick, and take a bite." Paolito enjoyed watching Mateo's anticipation.

Mateo ate. And ate. And laughed. And cried.

Paolito watched, almost forgetting to eat himself. He'd seen the same look on his son's face when he'd come home from military service ten pounds lighter than when he'd left home, only four months earlier. He was reminded of how his dear wife had always added salt before she tasted his meal. How it had bothered him, and now how he missed it so.

Mateo cleaned the last of the color from his plate with a piece of the bread Paolito had sliced from the morning's loaf. He drained the last glass of the ice-cold water, and lifted his plate to wash it at the sink.

Paolito used his conductor's arms once again to sit Mateo back down.

"I haven't had a guest in my home for so long, I thought I'd forgotten how to make flan."

Mateo's look of shock was the reaction Paolito had been going for, as he opened the refrigerator and pulled out a perfectly-formed flan, with caramelized sugar dripping from it.

"You didn't seriously make a flan in the time I was in the shed working," Mateo exclaimed.

"You were in there for four hours, you know." Paolito sliced the flan into quarters, and dismissed Mateo's unspoken resistance. "It's only good today and tomorrow, so we might as well get busy."

"I don't know how to thank you for all of this," Mateo responded quietly. "Really, this was the best meal I've had since

"Since you were sent to prison," Paolito finished. Mateo stepped back, with a look that Paolito recognized immediately as fear and suspicion.

"How did you know?"

Paolito stacked the two large plates and the dessert saucers before answering.

"There're only two reasons to have the look on your face you did when you ate that meal, and you're a little too old to be finishing your military service."

"If you want me to leave, I can go now," Mateo stammered, embarrassed to have been caught in his lie so quickly.

"Not on your life," Paolito replied, trying to put him at ease. "My son died in one of Castro's filthy prisons. I'm just glad you made it out."

"Well, I only SORT of made it out. They'll be looking for me, I'm sure. I wasn't supposed to make it home alive. Well, not home... where they have my sisters and nephew in Pinar del Rio."

Mateo decided it was more important that he clear the air with his host than return to the shop that night, and gave Paolito the Reader's Digest version of his life since he'd shared the proverbial cigar with Che Guevara. There were no tears, but definitely no laughter, either, as he recounted the treatment in the prisons, trying to water things down somewhat every time he saw Paolito react. He knew he was imagining how the last days of his son's life had been.

PART ELEVEN

It was nearly ten when he recounted the last encounter at the bridge, and how he'd narrowly escaped the same fate as his counterparts. He wanted Paolito to understand that he was putting himself at risk just by harboring him in his home.

Paolito approached Mateo, putting his two hands on the younger man's shoulders. "Listen to what I'm going to tell you right now. I'm the only child of my parents, and I had only one child. My wife of fifty-three years died in my arms when we received the news that our son had been captured and imprisoned. Thankfully she wasn't alive to see the sneer of the son of a bitch who came to tell us he'd been thrown into an unmarked grave for traitors."

Mateo just sat there, letting Paolito speak.

"Tell me what more they could possibly take away from me."

"Your home, everything." Mateo insisted he had plenty to lose.

"This?" Paolito almost screamed. "This was a home when I had a wife and a son, and they've been here half a dozen times to advise me that I should accept one of the apartments in Havana for old people without families. I only stay here to spite them."

"Can I ask you the names of your wife and son?" Mateo had a spark of an idea.

"My son's name was Angel, after his mother, Angela."

Mateo didn't say anything more. He asked Paolito for a blanket to sleep in the shop, and Paolito showed him to his son's room. There was a long look between them, and Mateo accepted the offer, knowing what it meant to the older man.

The soft mattress and feather pillow were too much for Mateo, though. After tossing for an hour, he gave up, and found a place big enough on the floor to lay down. Once he'd planned out his chores for the following day, sleep fell on him like a breaking wave.

Dreams of his sisters woke him in the night, and he stood by the window, listening to the sounds of a farm, and of freedom. He breathed deeply, finally allowing his nostrils to inhale to their fullest. The foul odors of hundreds of men in a confined space, with minimal facilities or water to wash had caused him to turn off that sense as much as he could for so many years. The trick of plugging one's nose to not taste foul medicine had become a permanent solution. If you smell it, it'll make you sick, they always warned the new guys. Think of your favorite food and chew fast and swallow.

There were horses nearby, Mateo could tell. They had a distinctive smell – almost sweet, and for him, especially. He'd ask Paolito in the morning. He heard more than one cat prowling near the window. He wanted to go outside and sit in the yard, but knew his movements in the house would disturb Paolito. It wasn't long before his system reacted to the strange food he'd ingested, and he made his way in the dark to the bathroom. He closed the door quietly before turning on the single bulb above the sink. Half of a Granma newspaper was folded next to the toilet. He knew reading anything in it would only infuriate him, but he couldn't help scan headlines boasting of the enormous success of the literacy program, the dozens of hospitals and schools that had been constructed, the records set in agricultural production. Using it to clean himself would feel good for more reasons than one. Once his stomach was returned to normal, he was able to sleep again, this time deeper than he could remember.

Five forty-five a.m., and Mateo's eyes sprung open. More than ten years of being forced to a routine of when he could use the bathroom, when he could eat, when he could exercise wouldn't soon be erased from his system. He tried to remain silent, but soon heard the rattle of pans and dishes from the kitchen. Apparently Paolito's inner clock had an alarm as well. Good, he thought to himself. He had a lot to do, and the day would be short enough.

"You're getting eggs and leftover chicken for breakfast, and no coffee." Paolito flicked a spatula in Mateo's direction. "You can drink coffee when you roast and grind some."

"Deal," said Mateo, grabbing the plates and cutlery to set the table. He noticed the fine table cloth had been replaced by a worn plastic one with faded flowers on it. He felt better about that, since he'd been self-conscious the previous night, worried he'd spill the reddish sauce on it.

"So I've been thinking about the situation here," began Paolito. "We need to figure out how to divide the chores."

"How about this: you cook and I'll do everything else that needs doing." Mateo slid two eggs onto each plate from the old frying pan.

"Until you can get around without that shovel handle, I think I'll continue to take care of the animals, and you get that coffee operation in shape. I've got people waiting for coffee, and besides, I haven't had a decent cup for three years, now."

Mateo caught himself shoveling his eggs and chicken, trying to keep within the ten minute time restraints of the prison. He was more than half done when he saw Paolito watching him, still savoring his first bite.

"Sorry about that," Mateo apologized. "Habits die hard."

"You don't worry about that, Son." There was an uncomfortable pause as both men realized what Paolito had just called him. "There's nobody here gonna rush you."

It made Mateo think about things his own father had said to him over the years. Things about how to act, how to treat other people, how to respect his mother and women in general. Having an older figure in his life didn't hurt him a bit.

Back in the workshop, Mateo was in his own world again. The oven was working and the roasting beans transported him to his father's place again. He traded in the crutch for a brace he fashioned from rags and wood, so that he had two free hands. He knew his shoulder had been damaged in the fall from the Jeep, too, and wanted to do something to bring the strength back to it. Out behind the shop was an inventor's playground, with pieces of wood and metal of all shapes and sizes. Naturally, Paolito had a small welder, and Mateo knew right away what he wanted to build himself. By lunchtime on the third day he was hanging from a chin bar that he bolted at the same height has his childhood one. He had cried out the first time he let his shoulder feel his weight, but he felt a snap as something moved into its rightful place, and he promised himself he'd be doing a hundred chin-ups before the end of the following week.

The horse, it turned out, was actually a large mule that Paolito had let wander the woods, fending for itself. His son had been the one to use the mule to carry coffee from the hills. Paolito preferred to haul a wagon. Mateo had a way with horses, too, and couldn't wait to get it strapped with baskets and head up to the source. "Just follow the trail – it's not more than a mile," Paolito had directed him. "I know you don't need my help to find coffee beans."

Mateo walked the beast along the trail, guiding it with kind words and gentle encouragement. He carried some sugar in his pocket, and gave her a taste once in a while, and before long the mule followed him like a puppy, her eyes concentrating on the sugar pocket. Just as he'd expected, the coffee plants were badly neglected, and almost choked out by undergrowth. This was going to take some time. Time, for better or worse, was what he had most of, considering he didn't exist.

He had sharpened the machete to a razor tip, and knew from years of experience how to hack everything but the coffee vines. He also trimmed the height of the bushes, so they would put more of their energy into producing beans and less into reaching for the stars, as his father taught him. "Keep your feet and your beans on the ground," his father had told him as a kid. It had sounded funny to him then, but there was more good advice in it than he had understood at the time.

He was surprised to find blisters forming on his palms after an hour of slashing and trimming. He took a five minute break and tended to the mule, finding a nice spot near a little creek where the grass was tender. He slid his tired hands into the cool water and scooped some over his head and face. It wasn't Topes de Collantes, but this was a fine place to live, he admitted.

He knew better than to keep Paolito waiting for the evening meal, so he reluctantly led the mule back down toward the house. It needed no coaxing to find its way home, and Mateo decided the next trip he'd try riding her. Far in the distance, another animal called out, and she responded with a shrill whinny. "That's what I'll call you," Mateo decided. "Whinny." He reached into his pocket, and asked her if she liked her new name. He decided she did, as she licked the sugar from his hand with her course tongue. "Next time, Whinny, you'll be carrying a hundred pounds of coffee beans to earn your sugar."

Paolito had another surprise waiting for Mateo when he finished his bath with hot water. It wasn't a special meal, this time, though. He had a pen and an old pad of paper on the table.

"Did I get the time wrong again?" Mateo asked, trying to make light of the strange turn of events. Normally there was a steaming pot of something waiting when he'd finished cleaning up.

"I need some information from you, and you're gonna have to trust me." Paolito sat down, picked up the battered pen, and held it as if ready to write a letter.

"What information are you talking about?" Mateo couldn't imagine what he knew that Paolito would want to know.

"We're only a couple of hours from Pinar del Rio, where you suppose your sisters are."

Mateo stiffened. This wasn't fun and games.

"But I can't

Paolito raised his pen to stop Mateo mid-sentence. "You can't, but I can."

Mateo's eyes betrayed him again. "It's too dangerous. They'll be watching them like hawks."

"That's why it's gotta be me. I have no connection to you or them. I'm just an old guy selling coffee, that's all. With my eyes and ears open, I should be able to find them quick enough. I remembered yesterday that I have a bunch of old pound bags from when Angel wanted to make his own brand of coffee to sell in the market. He never got the chance to fill the first one with coffee, though."

"I don't want you risking your life for me." Mateo tried to be firm, but Paolito had gone and opened up his box of hope.

"And I don't want you crying in the night and prowling around at all hours, either."

"But how would we do it so the secret police don't catch on?" Mateo's brain was working on different scenarios even as he asked.

"I thought we could come up with some kind of a code... something only your sisters would catch onto, like maybe a name they called you when you were little."

Mateo thought about that, and having been the oldest, he didn't think his sisters would remember any of the childhood names his parents had called him. "Wait... they know about how I can always tell what time it is, and about my grandfather's watch."

"There might be something there. Time... coffee... Coffee Time!" Paolito pounded his fist on the table.

"It's catchy, so nobody would suspect, but it might be too catchy for my sisters, too."

"Can you draw?" Paolito asked, looking into Mateo's eyes.

"It's not my strongest suit, but I've doodled a bit over the years."

"Can you draw your grandfather's watch? Is it recognizable to the girls?"

"They'd know it anywhere. It had an eagle's head on the cover."

"Then you better start drawing!" Paolito was proud of his positive action.

"But I can't help you with the money to get there. I have nothing."

"There's an oven in the shed that can make money, if there's a guy who knows how to use it properly."

"Aren't you gonna feed me, at least?" Mateo smiled and grabbed the pen and paper from Paolito's hands.

"I'll make you a sandwich when I see a watch and an eagle." There was more of Mateo's dad in this guy than he wanted to admit. He lovingly drew a pocket watch with the cover open, and tried to draw what his mind saw so clearly. Paolito set about slicing bread and the pork left over from the previous night's meal. He kept an eye on Mateo's progress as he worked. "Don't make it too complicated. We're gonna need to make about fifty of them to pay for the trip there and back."

The bags were top notch quality, Mateo saw, when he found them in the back of the shop, still in the original packaging. They were made to hold a pound of coffee, with a folding seal on the top that you could close again after the first time. They were made to be professionally printed, with a flat, smooth area on the front. His watch and slogan would fit nicely on these. He set about to make one with block letters and the watch on it, and decided it would serve their purpose.

When he had a bag he was satisfied with, Mateo set about to fill fifty of them with good quality ground coffee. He spent four hours rebuilding the ancient grinder that left too many course particles in the coffee. There were some rusted edges inside that made it impossible to grind uniformly. He filed them to a perfect finish, and sharpened the blades inside painstakingly, until he felt the powdery coffee grounds that would make the best espresso.

He carefully measured the first pound into the bag he had drawn, used a straw to syphon as much air from it as possible, and sealed it with the adhesive strip. He couldn't wait to show Paolito, and was through the door when he caught himself, and returned for enough coffee to make a pot, first.

Had he not returned for the coffee, he might have run straight into the two officials that accompanied Paolito, and were on their way to the coffee shed. Mateo did an about-face and headed for the tool room, where there was a door he could hide behind. Paolito spoke in a loud voice, doing his best to advertise their arrival. These were the same men who wanted him to give up the farm and move to the nice, comfortable old-folks home the government had refurbished from some fancy mafia properties they'd 'nationalized' at the start of the revolution. Of course, they would take the farm as trade for the apartment. After all, he wasn't really using it.

Paolito hadn't been back to the shop since Mateo had begun his overhaul, so he did his best not to look as surprised as the other two were when he opened the door, his eyes darting from corner to corner to see if Mateo had heard him in time. The first thing all of them saw was that it was completely spotless. Not a speck of dust or clutter anywhere.

"I see you keep your shop much tidier than your house," one of them pointed out.

"I don't plan to sell anything I prepare in my kitchen," Paolito responded, still in awe, himself.

"So you've suddenly taken a new interest in the coffee business." The second man seemed to be searching his memory for something. "Did you get a new oven?"

Paolito saw the way the man ran his fingers along the brick joints.

"I don't remember it being this well built."

"I took it apart and built it again. A guy came by and told me it was too tall."

"Smart guy," he continued, like a dog after a bone. "Who would this smart guy, be? I might want to consult with him myself."

"I don't recall his name. Black fella. About seventy years old. Knew a lot about coffee, that's for sure. Think he said he was from Santiago. Just stopped by one day, looking for work, so I got him to clean the place up and tell me how to fix the oven." Paolito did his best to steer them as far from Mateo as possible.

Mateo heard everything from behind the sliding door of the tool rack. He tried to think of anything that would give him away. Then he heard the first guy again.

"What the heck is that over there?" he pointed.

"What are you talking about?" Paolito was just trying to buy time, thinking of any idea to explain Mateo's chin-up bar.

"That pipe up there on the wall. It wasn't there before when we came here."

Mateo's heart sank. He considered stepping out and letting the cards fall where they may, when he heard an odd sound, like there was some kind of a scuffle.

Paolito, who was thirty years his senior, and thirty centimeters shorter, had summoned up a strength that surprised the two men, but possibly himself even more. There was a small block of wood near the area where the bar was, and the older man calculated in his head that if he got a running start, he could use the block to reach the bar, and launched himself up. His fingers nearly didn't reach to grasp the bar, but he found a way to sway to one side enough for his second hand to get a better grip. He was wiry thin, and had worked hard all of his life, but he couldn't remember the last time he had done anything that remotely resembled exercise. He lifted himself up to where his eyes were level with the bar, and held on for dear life. After an eternity of fewer than ten seconds, he lowered himself on his outstretched arms, looked down to ensure he wouldn't fall onto the block, and dropped, just barely maintaining his balance.

"The doctor says I need to do this three times a day, or I'll be in a wheelchair in a year." He pointed to his spine, and made a curved shape with his left arm. "Ostio something or other."

The two men seemed to accept his explanation, and moved on to other things. "Putting that damned thing up was harder than the exercise." One last detail.

Mateo breathed for the first time in what seemed like an eternity. He knew he owed Paolito big time for that personal sacrifice.

When the two men had accepted their "gifts" of packages of Mateo's latest grind of coffee and finally left the property, Paolito whistled an all-clear to Mateo, and leaned against the work bench to catch his breath.

Mateo was anxious to make sure the older man wasn't hurt from the exertion, and rushed to examine him.

"You okay, Paolito?" he asked, looking for signs of injury.

"Something cracked when I was hanging up there." The old man indicated his lower back on the left side.

"Do you need to sit down?" Mateo reached for the only chair in the room.

"I need to go dancing," Paolito responded, dancing a little jig for Mateo. "It's been years since I could stand up this straight."

The two men laughed until Paolito decided he'd worn out the joke.

"Well, Mateo, you need to get back to work. Those two jokers just hauled off half of the new production, and I found a ride to Pinar del Rio for the day after tomorrow."

Mateo scanned the workshop, and the piles of roasted beans to be sorted and ground, and the packages he had been doodling, trying to come up with a brand, and turned Paolito politely toward the exit. "Then you need to dance your Olympic athlete's body out of here and let me get to work."

Paolito pretended he was going to do a cartwheel, winked, and headed toward the house. "Dinner will be served at eight. Tie not required."

The car that would take Paolito to Pinar del Rio didn't look much like it would make it down the lane to the workshop. It had no side windows, and the right, front fender was held in place with baler wire. The headlight on that side drooped inward and toward the ground, looking for all the world like a sad puppy. Most of the car was a tone of green that wouldn't have come from any factory. There were brush marks, indicating it had been painted with leftover house paint. Mateo tried to imagine a house that color, but couldn't. He knew a lot more about horses than cars, so he couldn't identify the make or model, but he knew instantly that the day he could afford to buy a car, which would probably be never, that was the car that he didn't want to own.

Paolito shook the driver's hand and clapped him on the back, indicating they were good friends, and waved Mateo over.

Mateo was reluctant to leave his sanctuary of the shop, but the smile on Paolito's face assured him that there was nothing to worry about. He wiped the coffee dust from his hands onto the apron he'd been using, and approached the pair of friends.

"This is the guy I was telling you about, Julio… he makes the best coffee I've ever tasted."

"You've only had your own to compare it to," retorted Mateo. "And that's not a fair fight."

"I haven't had my coffee yet, today," responded Julio. "How about I be the judge?"

"I just poured a thermos for the trip," beamed Paolito, popping the plastic cup off of the ancient metallic jug, and pouring a generous amount of the steaming coffee. "Tell me this isn't a little slice of heaven."

Julio's eyes told them before he got a chance. The way he stood up straight and cocked his head to one side, and squinted, lips pursed, suggested he was looking for the right words. He refilled his mouth, and held it there for half a minute before he finally swallowed.

"I was trying to remember when I've tasted anything like that before, and I just remembered." He waited for Paolito to prod him for details.

Mateo enjoyed the satisfaction of knowing a non-objective third party had obviously approved.

"It was my first kiss, her name was Juanita, and she was an angel, to be sure, back in secondary school…"

Paolito slapped him on the back.

"And where is Juanita now?" Mateo quipped.

"She married my best friend, Roberto, and they have four children."

"So you had to be satisfied with just that one kiss, then," Paolito surmised.

"Well… they say his third boy has green eyes…" He winked at Mateo, making sure he could see the color of his eyes -- they matched his car. The three of them laughed again.

Mateo realized how good it felt to laugh, and his suspicions of Paolito's friend melted away. He could feel the tension drift out of his bones as he relaxed and allowed himself to enjoy a moment of levity between men, and knew he had one more person in the world he could trust. It was still a very short list.

The bags under Mateo's eyes were the biggest giveaway that he hadn't slept since Paolito had left the shop nearly 48 hours earlier. There had been so much to do, and he knew, somehow, that if the first batch hadn't been something special, his dream of reuniting with his sisters and having some semblance of his old life again would be over before they started. In order to be legitimate, he'd needed to package at least four dozen one pound containers of coffee, each with the label and logotype, and he'd had no copy equipment. He'd drawn and colored them one at a time, and they needed to be flawless. In the meantime, the oven had never stopped roasting and turning the coffee. He'd known by the smell when they were ready, and there was an art to grinding – it had to be fine and uniform in order to produce perfect espresso – other types of coffee were more forgiving. Draw, roast, grind, package, prepare, taste, adjust temperature, repeat. The first twenty-four hours had flown by. When he'd felt the fatigue setting in, he'd dropped to the floor and done fifty pushups and fifty more chin-ups on the bar. He could draw a label in under five minutes by the time he'd done two dozen. The hands on the watch always signaled 6:00 a.m., a typical coffee time for working Cubans.

While he worked, he wrote and rewrote the letter to his sisters in his head. There was so much to say to them, but he struggled to know where to start. He wondered if they'd even want to hear from him after so long, and after not being there for his mother. He didn't know if he should even bother to ask about Gladys. She'd have moved on years earlier, and probably had four kids running around her by then. He couldn't blame her – their marriage had never been consummated, and she had been young and fatherless. The most natural thing for her to have done was to have found someone to settle down with to help her mother.

He forced thoughts of Gladys from his head, tried to think of what to say about the loss of their mother, and tore up page after page of the precious little notebook he'd found to write the letter.

Paolito helped arrange the fifty-four packages of coffee into the spare tire compartment of the old relic of a car. Julio covered them carefully with plastic, and then lowered the thin wooden trunk liner into place, arranged half a dozen pieces of cardboard and old rubber mats on top of it, placed the spare tire on top of them, and sprinkled enough gasoline from the twenty liter jug to mask any coffee odor, in case they were pulled over. Few people trusted the poor quality rusted fuel tanks of the older cars. It was easier just to connect the hose directly from the plastic jug.

Paolito had the special package, with the hour and minute hands reversed on the logo, reading twelve thirty, safely tucked under the front passenger seat. The short letter from Mateo was folded neatly and covered in wax paper, in the center of the coffee, to be discovered days after he had been gone, so as not to draw suspicion to either party.

The old jalopy coughed to life, and Mateo wondered again if it could really make the trip, listening to the creaks and complaints from the heavy steel parts grinding against each other, sorely in need of grease. As it found the straight portion of the driveway with the grass growing down the middle, he noticed that the car never really straightened itself – the right-hand side of the car was more visible than the left. It was truly an essay in things that could be wrong with a vehicle. He watched until it sputtered and ground into second gear to turn right onto the secondary highway that would take them to the main highway that would eventually turn west towards the community of Pinar del Rio.

Mateo realized after a few minutes that he was alone for the first time in as long as he could remember, at least with nobody chasing him with guns. He decided to take the opportunity to fix some of the things he'd been embarrassed to do around Paolito, for fear of offending him. He'd noticed door hinges in need of adjustments, leaking taps in the kitchen and tub, and plenty more to keep his mind and body occupied for the next two days until the two men and their rolling junk yard returned.

The first thing he did, though, was pour the last drops of coffee from the thermos into the plastic lid and swish it around, noticing the color and texture and aroma. It wasn't his, yet, but it was as close as he could get it with the quality of the beans at this lower altitude. There was nothing to compare with the mountain air and humidity in Topes de Collantes. It was better not to dwell on those thoughts, though, because they could bring a storm of melancholy with them in the blink of an eye.

Before he started these chores, though, he wanted to put his own workshop back into order. He brushed the counters and table tops clean of coffee dust, pulled out the metal grates below the brick oven, and used the long bamboo-poled bristle broom to sweep the webs out of the corners.

There was still one pile of un-ground beans left over from the fifty-five one-pound packages he'd been able to prepare in the time he'd had. He finished sweeping the shop until it was as spotless as he liked to keep it. It was still mid-morning, but he could feel the muscles in his legs commanding him to rest. Something made him scoop his two cupped hands into the roasted beans and he buried his face into them and allowed himself to cry, finally. The gentle sobs became shoulder-jerking spasms that turned into a full-fledged muffled wailing. Beans fell onto the pristine floor as he let himself slide down the four-by-four posts onto the concrete. The rest he so badly needed turned out not to be in his bed, but surrounded by tear-moistened coffee beans.

PART TWELVE

The first to arrive in the resettlement communities found their homes, if you could call the tiny places homes, unfinished and uninviting. None had any paint on the inside, and the outsides were all bare blocks, with little effort made during construction to make the walls even straight, much less scrape the excess mortar that squeezed out when the blocks were pressed into place. There was no electricity in the apartment-style dwellings, nor water in the tanks on the roof. There was only a community well nearly a quarter mile from the nearest house, and it had an old hand-pump.

Isabel and her daughters and grandson had been among the first to arrive, with one bag each of clothing, supplies and any food they could scavenge. They'd been forced to share the back of the truck with three other father-less families, and four pigs and twenty chickens. Corina had immediately befriended one of the chickens and was entertained throughout the more than seven hour journey, during which they were provided no food or water by the young soldiers. Isabel had fiercely protected her daughters from the ever-prying eyes, and sometimes hands, of the soldiers. With no adult men to protect them, rapes and other sexual assaults had been common practice.

When they'd arrived at the construction site, they were herded toward the easternmost complex, and assigned apartment 1-C; they'd been the third family. The other two groups that had made the journey with them had been assigned 1-D and 2-A. If their conditions had been poor, they'd been lucky compared to the family in 2-A; there were still no doors or windows installed, and the woman had three children under five years old.

Isabel's first order of business had been to secure the door and window, so that she and Lisbet could make the trek to the well for water. Heidi would look after Corina and Juan and try to tidy the apartment as much as possible. One of the workers on the third floor had agreed to lend them an old broom, probably to avoid using it himself.

Finding anything that would be useful to carry back water had been a challenge. The Negro lady in 1-A had been there for nearly two weeks, and had already found anything useful within miles of the complex. She offered two old buckets, if we would bring one of them for her use. The woman in 1-B had a big cream container with a lid that she used, and she gave them the same offer. Water first, then they'd worry about how to cook the rice and beans they'd been able to carry with them.

While they'd been on their water pilgrimage, a truck had arrived carrying a few basic supplies. One cot per person, a few rudimentary cooking utensils, thread-bare towels – two per household, two live chickens, one bar of soap, a small bag of dirty rice, some black beans, and a bottle of milk for every child under seven years old. Lisbet had been told the pigs would be butchered the following day and the meat would be divided. Since there was no power, much less refrigeration, everything would need to be cooked immediately, or salted, to last the few days it would.

The question on everyone's mind was when there would be electricity. In 1-A and 1-B there were old refrigerators that had been delivered a few days after they'd arrived, obviously having been confiscated from other homes during the "cleansing" process.

On their walk to the well, Isabel and Lisbet saw the men laboring in the newly-tilled gardens, surrounded by barbed-wire fences. They were the ones who had either escaped the prisons, or had finished their sentences and been assigned to the labor camps to provide for the families. Isabel couldn't keep herself from scanning the faces to see if somehow her son had been moved. It had been years since she'd had contact with Mateo, and her pleas to know where he was being held were met with apathetic ears. She could recite their response from memory. 'I don't know where he is, and even if I did, I'm not authorized to give out that information.'

At the well, they met more of their new neighbors, and learned more about the life they could expect in the relocation community. Dirty rice, the broken beans that were left over when they were sorted for the general population – the sheep, as they were called by the non-revolutionists. Many at the well told stories of their deceased husbands, so Isabel counted her blessings. She may not have known where Mateo was, but she held onto the hope he was still alive, and that she would see him again one day. Some of the others had found wheels that they had used to make rolling carts to haul their water back to the village. Isabel and Lisbet found they couldn't carry their buckets and the cream can if they were full, so they had to empty nearly half of each into others' buckets. They would need to bring Heidi next time. She was stronger than Isabel. Once they'd divided the water with the neighbors, there'd be enough to drink, but their baths would be rationed dramatically.

The gloom was brightened significantly when they finally arrived home when little Juan raced toward them, proudly clutching the egg one of their two chickens had produced. Isabel smiled for the first time since they'd be herded onto the open truck to be relocated. Juan would enjoy "boneless chicken" tonight. The rest would have rice and beans – if Heidi had managed to scrounge enough twigs for a fire.

PART
THIRTEEN

Mateo pulled himself together and began to fix things around the house. Chairs, door hinges, leaking pipes and taps, roof tiles, lamps, discarded fans – once he started, he was on a mission. In the back of the tool cupboard, he found most of a gallon of paint. He didn't find a brush, but he knew where to find one – the mule wouldn't miss a few inches of her tail.

Paolito wouldn't recognize the place when he returned the following morning. Mateo knew that he'd need to pick up his pace if he wanted to accomplish everything he had planned. It wasn't lost on him that those two words had been all but erased from his vocabulary over the past ten years – accomplish and planned – he couldn't help but shake his head and smile at the thought.

Everything he repaired was a small repayment to Paolito for the acts of kindness and humanity he had shown to Mateo, and a small compensation for the loss of the son who would have done the same had his life not been taken by the same forces that had tried to extinguish his. His arms began to tire from the brush strokes of paint on the rough concrete walls. He mentally calculated the amount of paint still in the can, compared to the amount of wall left to paint, and knew it was going to be close. The trim around the windows would need to wait. He squeezed the remainder out of the tail-hair brush, satisfied that Paolito would be pleased, even though the last few feet were much fainter in color than the rest. There was a lime tree a dozen yards from the house, and Mateo pulled two ripe ones off to make himself a cool drink, while he pondered the next victim of his mission. While he knew it wasn't going to be any fun, the chicken coup had been crying out for a cleaning and fence mending. He briefly thought about tearing down the fence altogether, considering what it represented to him, but he decided against it, based on the fact that the treatment of the chickens, and the food they received every day were infinitely better than the conditions he had lived in.

PART
FOURTEEN

Paolito and Julio found the village in Pinar del Rio without much trouble. It was visible from the main highway, and the lack of anything resembling luxury – cars, bicycles, even toys, gave it away as a refugee camp more than a community. Most of the slatted windows had no curtains behind them, and few had anything but the dull whitewash color.

The first thought that passed through Paolito's mind was that his plan to sell coffee in order to find Mateo's family was going to flop long before it started. First, because it didn't look like the combined income of the three-story building in front of him could buy a package of coffee, and second, because the mere entrance of a non-military vehicle into the area had mobilized the green Jeeps into action.

They had to move slowly with the old car. Shock absorbers and springs were long-since discarded from the vehicle. Every little bump felt like a land-mine, shuddering the car and its occupants. The lack of private vehicles had made the need for roadways unnecessary. The four-by-four military trucks and Jeeps made their own.

A strange car entering from the highway was an excuse to find out how fast the Jeeps could go, it appeared, because there were two of them blocking Julio's advancement within thirty seconds of the old car having left the main thoroughfare. The barely-teenaged soldier in the first Jeep to arrive couldn't hide his enthusiasm for his job, bounding from the open door with his Russian rifle prominently displayed. Julio had to jam his left foot onto the emergency brake pedal to avoid coasting into a low-speed collision. The brakes on the car were just metal-on-metal, and made the nastiest music when the two met.

Julio reached above the sagging sun visor for the torn papers for his car, and his own papers – the first thing asked for when any civilian and authority met. He motioned for Paolito to leave it up to him. By the wear-marks on the visor, and the condition of the papers, it was obvious this was a frequent event.

He stepped out of the car, brushing his pant-legs into shape after the long drive. He felt good to be standing upright, and noticed a couple of vertebrae snap appreciatively. He handed the papers to the young soldier with his left hand, while holding up the coffee thermos with his right.

"Julio Gonzalez, at your service." He lifted the thermos toward the soldier, as an unspoken invitation. Accepted, he spun off the lid, and poured a little more than an ounce of the still-warm coffee. "We're here by permission of the newly-formed department of commerce to distribute coffee to the revolutionary soldiers, and to sell it to the civilian population to help pay for the costs."

The soldier had a skeptical look on his face as he held the coffee to his nose, first. He couldn't mask the surprise that came from the odor of something he hadn't encountered in a very long time. It was probably a memory from his own youth. He took the first sip, holding it in his mouth and moving it around for full effect. His eyes locked onto Julio's, looking for a sign that this was a practical joke. Julio moved his eyes from the soldier's to the cup, nodding his head almost imperceptibly, inviting him to confirm what couldn't possibly be true. An older soldier, more decorated than the first, arrived, and the look on the younger one's face returned to the somber, serious one of BC – "Before Coffee". He turned on his boots, saluted the senior officer, and realized he still had the plastic thermos lid in his left hand.

The senior man dismissed the younger, and turned his attention to Julio.

"Captain Jimenez: they're here to give us coffee and sell it to the civilians." He lifted the cup as though it was proof of what Julio had invented minutes earlier. "Try this coffee."

The senior started to say something, but caught the scent as the cup was thrust at him. He took it from the young soldier and signaled with his eyes for him to retreat to his vehicle. He would handle it from then on. As the younger man retreated, the older one relaxed his demeanor. He lifted the cup to his mouth and emptied it in one quick motion, swallowing it without hesitation.

He glanced down at the papers he'd grabbed from the retreating subordinate's hand. "Now, Julio Gonzalez, tell me what you're REALLY doing here, because there is no such thing as a coffee salesman in this Revolution."

Paolito had been watching the scene play out from inside the car, and knew he was about to get his friend into a world of trouble if he didn't do something. He had to nearly fracture his right shoulder in order to coax the door open, causing all eyes to shift to him and where the creaking had come from.

"It's okay, Julio. I think I should tell him the truth." The look on Julio's face told him they were both going to be in a world of trouble if he did. The official had a satisfied look on his face. He had caught them in their lie with his experience and wisdom. "I'm looking for my grandson. My son is dead, and he had a son, and I heard he was living here, so I packaged some of my coffee to try to sell it to pay for the gas to get here to find him.

Jimenez cocked his head, still skeptical. "You're still trying to tell me that this coffee is yours?"

"Well, it was my son's business, but I'm trying to keep it alive in his memory. That's what the watch on the package is for. He was born December 30th – that's why the watch is stopped at twelve thirty. And he was always telling me it was coffee time, so that's why I chose that name."

"Give me another taste of your coffee, and tell me why you think this lost grandson of yours is here." He held the thermos lid back to be refilled, and examined the hand-drawn logo and branding on the package Julio had fetched from the trunk. "I know every family living here, and I've never heard any of this before, and believe me, I hear everything."

"It's because I just found out in a letter my son left me when he died." Paolito was making it up as he went along, but the hint of an actual plan was forming in his mind. "All he told me was that he had a son named Juanito – my son's name was Juan, after my father – and that the mother's name was Lisbet. He'd never been married to her, so he doesn't have our last name.

The captain paused mid-sip at the mention of the names Lisbet and Juanito. He could end the charade in a moment. They lived in Building I-C, not four blocks from where they were standing. They'd been among the first to arrive, and had been under constant vigilance – orders directly from Pomares. No explanation had been given, and in the more than five years they'd been in the village, they'd had no visitors or contact with anyone that he knew of. Lots of the soldiers had done their best to coax either Lisbet or Heidi, to no avail. Their mother, Isabel, while she was alive, was meaner than a hornet. She'd passed on several months earlier, so there was renewed hope the door might open for one of them. He had all of the feminine attention he could handle, already, what with the power to increase or decrease rations at will, but they were two of the best-looking women in the area. The loonie-toonie sister was a bit of a deterrent, though. She was always between her sisters and anyone who even tried to get close to one of them. Juanito had to be nearly ten or eleven years old by now, he calculated. He was about the age of his own son from his second marriage. He'd never heard of a father in the picture… just the uncle who'd been in prison and was shot escaping.

"You're welcome to take a package of the coffee with you, if you like it. I'm just trying to recoup the gas." Coffee was one of the staples of any Cuban's household – rice, beans, garlic, onions, sugar, cumin, and espresso coffee. People were judged by the quality of their coffee, and giving a gift of a particularly good-tasting grind could facilitate promotions.

"Make that two, every time you come this way, and I'll remember where Lisbet and Juanito live, and let you sell all the rest to pay for your gas." He had two households to maintain, and he wanted this coffee at both his wife's and girlfriend's places. He indicated to Julio to deposit them under the seat of his Jeep.

Julio made sure both packages shared the right hour, and nodded the confirmation to Paolito. The captain had already swallowed the second serving of coffee, and told them to follow him as he turned toward the four-wheel-drive. Back in their car, the two men shared a wordless celebration. They'd found the right person without even trying. He would take them straight to Mateo's family, without them having to pretend to find them by accident. Paolito turned the special package over in his hands. He had little time to figure out the next episode in his fairy tale – convincing Lisbet to go along with his story.

PART FIFTEEN

The suspense of not having any way to communicate with Paolito was eating Mateo alive. The potential for disaster was every bit as great as the possibility of success – much greater, actually. Everything in Cuba was controlled, and coffee was no exception. He'd learned that since the Castro regime had been in power, even the sugar trains had been patrolled by armed soldiers. The rationing was so strict that even in a country where sugar was more abundant than fresh air, people had been known to pry open the train car hoppers when they were stopped, to steal sugar to sell or trade on the growing black market. Getting caught with dozens of packages of unauthorized coffee could earn both Paolito and Julio a one-way ticket to a place like Mateo had recently been relieved from. He shuddered at the thought. He know Paolito would never survive a month.

There was nothing he could do but wait, though. Paolito didn't own a telephone, even if there was one where his sisters lived. He'd learned a little bit about patience over the past ten years, so he did what he always did when he wanted time to pass quickly – he found another project to occupy his time and his mind. The horse needed to be tended to, and the little shed it used for shelter looked like it might crumble with the next breath of wind. It had never been braced properly, and Mateo had seen some four-by-four timbers and a hand saw just a day earlier.

PART SIXTEEN

Pomares threw open his eyes and called out something unintelligible, drenched in sweat. He'd been having that dream again lately. It started differently almost every time, but always ended up the same way – with strong fingers around his throat. This was no way for a high-ranking officer in Castro's regime to be acting, and he waved off the offer of help from his worried wife. He pivoted himself to a seated position and used his pillow to wipe the moisture from his neck and face, tossing it onto the floor next to the squeaking floor fan. He kept meaning to requisition a newer one, but his wife said she didn't know if she could sleep without the familiar rhythm. It was another excuse for him to stay at his mistress' apartment two or three nights a week. She had a high-speed ceiling fan that he liked much better. He made his way to the bathroom and splashed water onto his face and neck, drying himself with the least thread-bare towel that hung from the fishing line outside the door. Any towels left in the humid bathroom smelled like filthy armpits in less than a day.

He heard his wife moving things in the kitchen. Coffee before anything else. Rule number one in Cuba, before, during and after the Revolution. The military officers were provided a significantly larger quota of staples than civilians, and the higher the rank, the sweeter the pot. If a regular soldier received a dozen eggs and three kilograms each of rice and beans, Pomares' package was triple that, with generous extras like beef instead of a few pieces of chicken. He heard the sizzle first, then the scent of fresh ham being fried with the four eggs he liked every morning. Adults weren't allotted milk in the general population, but Pomares had been a country boy, and had pulled a few strings to receive the allotted amount as though he had three small children, even though his own were far older than the seven years the party had arbitrarily set as the upper age limit for receiving it. What was the use of having stripes on his shoulder if he couldn't use them once in a while, he justified to himself. Milk and a few extra bottles of Havana Club Añejo rum. He'd started out telling himself it was good to have some on hand in case he entertained someone as important as himself, but later just gave in to the reality that he liked to finish his days with a few shots to help him to sleep.

Lately, though, he found himself waking up in his chair in front of the television with an empty bottle still in his hand. He knew it was becoming a problem when he'd pissed himself trying to get up to use the bathroom a few days earlier. He'd changed into a fresh uniform in the morning and hid the trousers and underwear in a bag that he tossed into a garbage on his way to work the following day.

Pomares found his way to the bathroom to splash water onto his face – he needed to get this under control. The stained mirror had a bit of a distortion to it, and made it hard to see himself properly. This didn't bother Pomares, though, because when he saw himself in a proper mirror, the deep scar over his right eye always reminded him of his weakness, and of the person who had given it to him. The records showed Mateo was dead – victim of an unfortunate traffic accident – but they'd never brought him the proof he'd ordered them to provide.

He knew the bastard was still out there. That was why he couldn't get a proper night's sleep, and looked over his shoulder more than a normal person ever would.

PART
SEVENTEEN

Lisbet was alone in the house when she heard the sound of vehicles approaching. Not many ever ventured over to Building One without a good reason, given that the road was never graded that far. No one had a car, or even bicycles around there, so she wiped her hands with the dish cloth she'd been drying the lunch dishes with, and adjusted the aluminum window slats so she could see down to ground level.

Lisbet recognized Captain Jimenez' Jeep right away. It was the newest one in the community, and he always made sure it was spotless. She felt a tingle of unease at the fact that her sisters were visiting friends in Building 36 – they were from Trinidad, and knew some people in common. Juanito didn't finish school until four in the afternoon, so this was Lisbet's time to organize the place and if there was time, watch a little of the afternoon soap opera. They were playing one from Brazil, and she loved to imagine living the life of luxury the characters in the soaps did.

She noticed the other car as it came into view from the angle of the window. It was civilian, she noted, making it something she'd be able to tell her sisters about. Anything other than an army Jeep was news-worthy and broke the monotony. She'd make note of the make and color so she could tell them about it. She wondered who they were visiting. She'd be sure to slip out and walk past their place, so she could try to hear what was going on.

She was more than a little surprised when the vehicles stopped almost directly in front of her own door. Her first thought was maybe something had happened to the grandmother next door. She'd slipped and broke her hip a month earlier. Maybe they were bringing a doctor to examine her at home.

It was even more unusual that the footsteps didn't slow their pace as the three men walked past the door of I-D, and stopped directly in front of hers. She almost jumped out of her skin when the sharp knock confirmed they were actually looking for someone in her home. A hundred thoughts assaulted her mind as she automatically stepped back from the kitchen window and unconsciously made an inventory of all of the things that were out of place in her house, and caught herself flattening the wrinkles of her ancient dress. Had something happened at the school? Had Juanito gotten into another fight, or worse, had he been hurt? Was it something to do with one of her sisters? The beef hidden in the back of her freezer suddenly screamed to be discovered. That was a huge problem – but Juanito needed more protein than he was getting, and didn't like beans. Lisbet thought briefly about flushing it down the toilet, but knew it would only plug the pipes and she'd be in even bigger trouble.

All of these thoughts happened while she walked the five feet from the kitchen window to the front door.

She opened the door wide enough to expose Captain Jimenez' face. His expression didn't suggest anything urgent. And for once he didn't rest his eyes on her cleavage, so that was a bonus.

"Good afternoon, Captain Jimenez." Lisbet knew she needed to always be respectful of the military. Every little thing was written in their endless reports, especially the level of enthusiasm each family displayed at any Revolutionary celebration. And there were endless excuses for rallies. Everybody with a brain knew that Camilo Cienfuegos had been "erased" because of his vocal discontent at the Russian alliance, but Fidel was smart enough to make him a martyr, and have all of the children on the island learn songs in his tribute. "A flower for Camilo, in the water we will toss…" Juanito had worn out more than one pair of shoes trudging the five kilometers to the nearest river with his classmates, carrying a wilted flower the entire way, just to toss it into the stream and come back. "Is there something I can do for you?" She regretted giving him such an opening, given his reputation and past insinuations toward her and Heidi. He'd made some rude comments about Corina that she'd fought the urge to respond to, as well.

"I'm not here on a social call," Captain Jimenez responded, using his important man voice. "I bring you visitors from near Havana. Luckily I knew just where to find you."

Lisbet's reaction made it clear she had no idea what he was talking about, and as she opened the door wider, she obviously showed no sign of recognition for the two strangers behind him.

Captain Jimenez smelled something out of the ordinary, and was determined to flush out the culprit if this was some sort of trick. He actually had studied such a thing in his officer training a few years earlier. The professor had been some kind of KGB agent from the Soviet Union, and he could ferret out a lie better than anyone Jimenez had ever met.

"I should introduce myself, I suppose, because we've never met, although my son spoke of you often before he…" Paolito didn't need to fake the emotion associated with the loss of his only son. That came without any coaxing. After so many years, anything could set him off – the scent of mint reminded him of how much his son loved the garden. A crack of thunder would remind him of how, as a little boy, he would curl up in the corner of his room with his hands covering his ears. If he saw the particular shade of green that was his favorite, a tear would always follow. "My son, Juan, was a very good friend of your brother, Mateo, and"

Lisbet's attention came to an abrupt crescendo at the mere mention of her brother's name.

"You knew my brother?" She searched his eyes for a clue. This was starting to sound a little too surreal for her.

Paolito knew he had very little time to get her onto his train of thought, or she'd expose his lies without knowing his motives.

"Your son's name is Juan, am I right?"

Lisbet nodded, but didn't give him much more rope. Only a couple of people in the world knew the identity of her child's biological father, and this old stranger definitely wasn't one of them. "That's no secret. He's nearly eleven years old, but we still call him Juanito."

Captain Jimenez decided to move the show along. "Lisbet, this guy says he's Juanito's grandfather, and that his son gave him your information on his dying bed. It sounds to me like his story is as much of a surprise to you as it was to me. Do you want me to ask him to leave?"

Lisbet cocked her head to one side, trying to make sense of what she was hearing. She knew that the father of the man who had raped her so many years ago had died since of prostate cancer. She still got news from Topes from time to time. So who was this man, and why had he mentioned her dead brother? She was about to agree to the captain's suggestion, when the third man, who hadn't said a word to that point, held up a bag of something with his finger pointing conspicuously at the drawing of a man's watch. He hid the gesture from the captain, by keeping the first man's body between him and the bag.

"Could we at least interest you in some coffee?" The third man tried to diffuse the situation, but Lisbet wasn't biting his pantomime, still pointing at the watch on the bag.

"The guy who taught us to blend the coffee so well has a special penchant for time," interjected Paolito. "He can tell exactly what time it is at any moment of the day, without ever looking at a clock. It's uncanny, don't you think, Miss Lisbet?"

That one hit its mark. Lisbet knew immediately that this man was referring to her brother, Mateo. Now, to figure out what the heck he was talking about. She knew she needed to play along, to keep Jimenez from catching on.

"Now I remember! Your son mentioned you a few times. Why don't you come in out of the sun and I'll make some coffee?"

Paolito knew he'd convinced her that he knew more than he was letting on. "Please try the coffee we brought, so you know what we're talking about."

Captain Jimenez was anxious to confirm that the coffee they were selling was of the same quality as what he'd tasted earlier. His reputation might depend on it. "Yes, Lisbet, please try some of their coffee."

Paolito shot a look at Julio, who confirmed with an almost-imperceptible nod that the bag he held in his hand was indeed the special one, meant for Lisbet's eyes only. Mateo had been careful enough to place his letter deep inside the package, so it wouldn't be accidentally exposed during the first or second pot. It might even take a few days before it would surface. He had known that after ten years, two or three days more wouldn't do any more damage.

Lisbet took the time to carefully clean the aluminum coffee maker, to give the new blend a chance to prove itself. She knew there was something about the coffee she needed to learn. Her painstaking cleaning gave her a moment to think about some of the possibilities of what these men were saying. Could it be possible that Mateo hadn't been killed in the accident, if it actually was an accident? Why hadn't he been in touch with her and the others? Where was he now? Was he hurt? Was he in trouble?

Captain Jimenez brought Lisbet back to the present with a loud, conspicuous clearing of his throat. He had other things to attend to, and wanted this charade to be over one way or the other. She caught the message, and began to fill the coffee maker with water.

Paolito opened the bag, and glanced quickly inside to make sure there was nothing visible. He feigned filling his nostrils with the aroma of the fine coffee, and handed it to Lisbet. "This package is free, for you, for being our first customer. If you like it, tell your friends and neighbors. If you don't like it, tell me."

"It smells almost as good as my father and brother used to prepare in Topes de Collantes," she responded. "You can't beat the mountain climate for growing perfect coffee beans."

"Ah, somebody knows their coffee, I see." Julio took the initiative to wipe out four tiny cups, and placed them on the counter. "I want to make sure there's no taste left from the competition." They all shared a laugh, which was exactly what was needed to diffuse the tension.

PART
EIGHTEEN

Mateo wiped his forehead with his left arm, smearing sweat and straw and excrement from his elbow to his wrist. The little shelter looked like it would make it to the next decade without any trouble, now that there was enough support for the adobe tiled roof. Paolito would be pleased, but not as pleased as Whinny, the off-white mule. The floor was a foot lower, too, now that he'd cleared the years of old straw and everything that went with it and piled them outside to use in the garden for fertilizer. He estimated there was about as much buildup as time had passed since Paolito's son had been there to help him.

He knew exactly what time it was, and consequently the noise his stomach was making reminded him that he hadn't had a bite since the evening before. He'd brought eight eggs in earlier, and there was some ham in the refrigerator. Mateo knew he needed to eat, or he'd collapse in the hot sun. He found a suitable place to store the pitch fork and was about to leave the shed when he heard the sound of a car motor approaching. He was surprised that Paolito and Julio could have been back so quickly. They should just be in Pinar del Rio now. He had calculated and recalculated the time to get there, find his sisters, and get home, and he knew it shouldn't be before nightfall. It was when the engine shut off before the vehicle got near the driveway that Mateo started to feel like something wasn't exactly right. When he heard the two doors close with the solid click of vehicles without broken hinges like Julio's, he decided he needed to find a place to hide and observe.

It was nearly five minutes before Mateo spotted the two men approaching the property. They had left the road for the cover of the row of flowering trees to the west side. Mateo had only seen them through the crack in the door of the workshop, but he recognized the two of them from their size difference and one had the same distinctive jacket with a patch on the sleeve, identifying him as an official inspector.

With the advantage of the shadows, Mateo stayed close to the side of the house, out of sight of the approaching men. He knew they weren't here for any surprise inspection, this time. They wouldn't have left their vehicle so far from the house and workshop. He could only think of two reasons: they were here to steal the coffee or other valuables they had seen on their previous trip, or they were on another mission, looking for a wanted fugitive. They must have been watching the place since their last time, and wanted no witnesses this time around.

The mule shuffled and snorted from the newly-repaired shed, probably aware of the unwelcome guests. Animals had a way of sensing when things were out of sorts – be it an approaching storm, or just negative vibes. Mateo's internal calculator estimated their arrival at the yard, based on the distance he had seen them from, and the relative walking speed through the thick grass and brush. He made a mental note of the conditions in the workshop. He had swept it the evening before, and had been sketching more bags for the next batch. He estimated there were fifty pounds of ground coffee in the two closed sacks sitting beside the scale. Not a giant haul for thieves, he noted. If they'd seen the tool cabinet, though, there was a target worth their trouble.

Within five minutes, he could hear their approach, and muffled conversation. They either assumed the place was abandoned, or didn't care.

PART
NINETEEN

Pomares had barely finished wiping his boots to a shine when a knock on the door startled him. He wasn't expecting anyone, and had been hoping to slip over to his mistress' apartment before going to the detachment to approve orders for the following week. He was surprised to see two junior officers standing at attention when he opened the door. At first he thought they were bringing him some message or other about a change in the planning meeting, but the fact that neither of them would look him straight in the eyes told him it was something else.

"At ease, soldiers," Pomares said, breaking the silence. They didn't relax their positions of attention, though.

"Sergeant Pomares, you are under arrest and have been cited for trial at the military court in Havana, Wednesday afternoon at sixteen hundred hours. We have been instructed to accompany you."

The sergeant's eyes and open jaw told the story of his surprise and shock. "What are the charges against me? This is an outrage! I'll have your jobs, and everyone else's who are behind this." He did his best to inflate himself to his full stature, and glared at the two junior men.

"Our instructions are to escort you to Havana without delay."

"I'll take this up with Fidel Castro himself." Pomares wanted them to know he had a personal relationship with the president and commander.

"I'm certain you will, Sergeant Pomares. The Commandante gave us the orders directly."

The deflation was immediate and obvious, and Pomares knew there was no point in resisting. If Fidel Castro wanted to see him, there was no denying the request, but why was he under arrest? "Can I pack a few things for the trip? How long will I be in Havana?"

"You cannot, and we have no idea of the duration. Whatever you require will be provided." The taller of the two soldiers did most of the talking. The shorter one stepped aside and turned ninety degrees all in one motion, and indicated with his eyes for Pomares to pass between them. As he turned to lock the door behind him, the taller man held his hand up to confirm it wouldn't be necessary. "There is an order to search your premises. The team is waiting downstairs. You can leave the key with them. Your property will not be left without a guard until you return."

Pomares' mind raced to what might be found that could be used against him. He recalled the box of empty rum bottles, and the case of full ones under the sink in the kitchen. Not very becoming of a senior officer in Fidel's army, but nothing to incriminate him, either. He nearly stumbled on the first step on his way down to the main level. It was a full two inches taller than the rest of the steps. He'd always meant to bring that up with the minister in charge of construction, but had never gotten around to it. There were two large and menacing guards framing the rear door of the enclosed Jeep. They had Russian machine guns in their grasp, and made a point of looking like they were more than ready to use them. The door was already open, and Pomares took no extra time in climbing inside. The entire neighborhood appeared to have assembled, on balconies, enjoying the show. Not many of them had fond sentiments for the boisterous sergeant, showing off his position and impunity at every opportunity. With all of the extras he carried into his apartment, he never once offered a morsel to the less fortunate around him, and was often course and crude toward the children who liked to run and play in the stairwells. In Cuba, people learned early and well not to voice their opposing opinions, but there was another entire language that comprised of hand gestures and eye rolling and even little clicks of the tongue that had meaning among friends and neighbors. There were plenty of these winks and nods and clicks going on, mostly confirming that they were happy to see a big shot being knocked from his high horse. Lots of subtle nods that confirmed from one balcony to another that they always knew he was bad, deep down, and it was good that he was going to pay for his sins, whatever they were.

As it turned out, Fidel Castro had taken some serious advice from his Russian counterparts, installing checks and balances on every level, weeding out anyone who worked against him or the system. He had KGB agents from Russia training his secret police with what to look for, and how to blend into the society so that even family members didn't suspect them. Fidel was an avid reader and student to Mao Tse Tung and his regime in China, and developed a strong network of informants, beginning with the CDR's – Committee for the Defense of the Revolution. A brilliant orator and charismatic genius, Castro could convince the masses that everything he did was for their benefit, and that they all had a common enemy in the evil Americans, so everything he did to keep such tight control was for their own good. And one of the things he learned from his Russian and Chinese counterparts was that punishing an insider publically could bring huge benefits from the masses in terms of loyalty and credibility.

Pomares saw some of the faces of his neighbors as he stooped to sit in the back of the Jeep. He saw them as pathetic losers, living so far below him he could barely acknowledge their presence. He had risen through the ranks, and had dined at Fidel Castro's table. He was confident he would sort this mistake out quickly and get back to what he loved – being powerful.

He also began to plan revenge on whoever it was who had accused him. They would pay dearly, he was certain.

PART TWENTY

Lisbet made sure not to draw any additional scrutiny from the captain, but she knew there was more that the older man wasn't able to say to her. The story he told about his son was far from true, but still she could tell he had no bad intentions, and it seemed pretty clear that he had some knowledge of Mateo. But how? She had been given the news personally by Captain Jimenez himself of the accident and how Mateo had died before he could be taken to a hospital. They even had a ceremony for him and one of the other men in the vehicle whose family was in the same complex as she was. Both of their bodies had been cremated and brought to the families within a few days of the accident.

Paolito could sense her skepticism and wanted to leave her with something more. He was painfully aware of the captain's eyes burrowing into him at every moment, so he thought it better to cut the visit short, to diffuse the situation.

"Remember the name of the coffee, so you don't confuse it with others," he offered, trying to focus her attention on the package. "It's the only one with a pocket watch, with an eagle on it."

Lisbet picked up the bag again. "It looks like it was drawn individually."

"Yes, every bag is drawn personally. The artist loves his pocket watch. He told me it was handed down from his grandfather to his father, and then to him. Unfortunately, it was taken from him when he was imprisoned." He thought he should stop there, knowing the captain wouldn't appreciate discussion of political prisoners in his presence.

"It's time to get going," Captain Jimenez interjected. "You'll want to get on the road before it's much darker." His body language told them he was anxious to be rid of them.

"Is there a store where we can leave the rest of the coffee, to help us pay for the gasoline?" Julio tried to remind everyone they were there to sell all of the coffee, not one package.

"I'll instruct the person who runs the shop two blocks from here to take it off your hands at a reasonable price." The captain had the solution to get them on their way.

"Thank you, Captain." That would be a big help.

The three men made their brief good-byes to Lisbet, and headed for their respective vehicles. "Follow me to the store," the captain instructed coldly. He'd already arranged his cut, so he had no interest in wasting more time. As he started the Jeep, he glared once more at Lisbet, undressing her with his eyes. She saw his intention and stepped inside the apartment, closing the door behind her.

PART
TWENTY-ONE

Mateo tried hard to make out the conversation of the two approaching men, but they spoke softly, and were still too far away to read their lips. He noticed, though, that they carried nothing with them. In Cuba, everyone knew that if you wanted to transport anything at all, it was crucial to bring your own bag, because they were as uncommon as the food or other goods. A man who didn't have a plastic bag protruding from his hip pocket was a poor provider for his family.

They reached the yard in front of the house, and although they walked carefully, they didn't seem to be hiding or sneaking anywhere. He slipped around the corner of the shed as they neared the front door of the house, to maintain his advantage. The taller of the two actually knocked on the door, probably to prove what he already knew, that Paolito wasn't home.

"Mateo, you can come out from wherever you're hiding," called the smaller man in a loud voice. "We know you're here, and we have an urgent need to speak with you."

Mateo's heart hit the inside of his ribs with a thump at the sound of his name being called. How could they know he was here, and why weren't they carrying automatic weapons with a dozen soldiers flanking them? He thought about Paolito and Julio. Had they turned him in for some reason? He dismissed the idea as quickly as it came to him. He knew Paolito wouldn't have done anything to harm him, and Julio seemed equally trustworthy.

As though he had anticipated Mateo's very thoughts, the smaller one spoke again, just as loudly as before. "We knew it was you from the moment we entered the coffee workshop."

Mateo cocked his ears to listen closely.

"You made it the same as your shop in Topes de Collantes, and the chin-up bar was the final piece of the puzzle."

"We're not really inspectors for food and beverage," added the taller man. "We're with the justice department."

Mateo's sore leg suddenly gave out, and he slid down the side of the workshop to a seated position. Back to prison. He almost felt relieved at the idea of not hiding anymore.

"We've been investing crimes committed by Sergeant Ruben Pomares against the Revolution, and we are in need of your help."

Mateo's head shot up from where his chin had been resting on his chest. What did he just hear? Investigation, Pomares? Impossible. It was a trick, probably instigated by the sergeant himself.

"I have a written and signed pardon with your name on it." The shorter one again.

"Come on out and we can show it to you. We're unarmed and we know we're no match for you, Mateo. You have nothing to be afraid of, and besides, why would you continue to hide when now you know that your hiding place has been discovered. You'd only bring more problems for Paolito, and you wouldn't want him serving a sentence for harboring a fugitive."

Mateo stood up again, wiping at his welled-up eyes. The thought of Paolito being in trouble because of him was more than he could bare. If it was a trick, it was a well-executed one. They knew his weak spots.

"I'm coming to you," Mateo heard himself saying, pushing himself out into the open, almost waiting for guns to be drawn. None were. "Show me the papers."

The taller man nodded to the shorter one, who reached into his breast pocket, staring straight at Mateo, probably looking to see if he had a weapon in his hands himself. He slowly pulled out the folded papers and offered them in Mateo's direction.

Mateo's mind flashed back to the prison yard, and the food, and the inhuman treatment as he exposed himself to these strangers. He could see the look on Pomares' face as he leveled the rifle at him so many years ago on the winding road to Topes. He knew he wouldn't miss the next time. Better dead than back there, he decided, and relaxed his gait as he walked into the dimly-lit area in front of the house. He'd meant to change the bulb over the front door with something stronger. Now he wouldn't have a chance.

The shorter man stepped forward toward Mateo as he approached, the papers his olive branch. The taller one retreated, to ensure it didn't look like an ambush. He signaled Mateo to take the papers before speaking another word.

Almost reluctantly, Mateo reached out for the papers, still half-expecting a set of hand-cuffs to come out of nowhere. As he grasped them, the shorter man also stepped aside, leaving him alone in the dim light to read the document. He turned his back to the door of the house and leaned against it for support. He let his eyes leave the men for the first instant, and focused on the document in his hands. The quality of the paper was the first thing he noticed. It was thick and bright white, not the rice paper the Cuban people had become accustomed to since the Revolution, and there were no stains on it like all of the other letters he'd received, so many years earlier, having been passed from hand to hand a dozen times before they reached him.

He had just started reading the contents when his eye was drawn to the letterhead at the top of the page. Ministry of Justice of the Cuban Revolution, with an address in the best part of Havana. The lettering was raised and embossed, so it was clearly not a copy. And the wording was very professional, clearly written by lawyers. Without glancing up at the men, he read the two pages in their entirety, and was equally surprised to see that the document was copied to the office of the Commander Fidel Castro Ruz. Right to the top. When he had finished, he looked over the top of the pages to confirm with his eyes that what he was reading was true.

"You're officially a free man, Mateo, with all of the rights of any Cuban citizen. All that is asked of you is that you appear at the trial of Sergeant Pomares."

"And what do you want me to say at the trial?" Mateo felt a tightening in his belly at the idea of testifying in front of the court that never gave him the benefit of the same.

"One of the soldiers ordered to kill you and the others has confided that they were given instructions directly from Pomares. He's currently in custody in Havana, and has identified the others who were also present that day. He's the one who tipped us off that you were never really captured or shot. We put two and two together when we saw the conditions in the coffee shed here. We've been waiting for the sergeant to be taken into custody before we returned, just in case he had informants that we didn't know about inside our department." The tall man spoke easily and candidly, clearly aware of the injustices that Mateo had lived.

"We spent some time in Topes de Collantes, interviewing people who knew both of your families before you were imprisoned, and we've concluded there was no specific proof of counter-revolutionary behavior or activity on your part. Enough people advised us of the personal feud between you to allow us to form our conclusion."

"And after the trial, what happens to me?" Mateo felt his stomach relax just slightly, beginning to actually allow hope to enter his mind.

"Your plantation has been allowed to return to its original state after so many years of little or no attention, and the revolution has taken possession of the titles of all agricultural properties."

"So you're saying my farm isn't my farm anymore." Mateo wasn't at all surprised by the news, but there had been a seed of hope sewn, nonetheless.

"We're suggesting that given your obvious abilities with coffee," the shorter one interjected, waving his hand toward the coffee shed behind Mateo, "we might be able to use your expertise on a much larger basis, to help bring the Cuban coffee industry back to the standards necessary for international export."

"Work for the government of Cuba?" Mateo shook his head at the very idea. "After they kept me locked up for more than ten years... I don't think that's gonna happen."

"That's your choice. What ISN'T your choice is coming with us to testify against Sergeant Pomares, so that he can be made an example of for all of the Cuban people." The taller man once again referred to the document, and with just a slight nod of his head and a half wink, made the point that it was time to go.

"I'll need to pack a bag, get a change of clothes." Mateo knew from experience that there was no good to come of resisting.

"You can pack a bag if you like, but we have instructions to provide you with everything you require – clothes, shoes, food and lodging. The trial begins in two days, so we need to begin to prepare immediately." The shorter man tossed the keys to the taller one, and signaled for him to fetch the car.

Clearly he was the senior of the two. The taller one caught the keys and nodded his compliance, heading toward the main road where the car had been stashed.

Mateo looked down at what he was wearing, and decided it was as good as he had. "Let me just leave a note for Paolito, so he won't worry when he returns and I'm not here."

"Again, not necessary. He'll be advised upon his return from his coffee run to Pinar del Rio." He couldn't help but smile at Mateo's reaction to his revelation that they knew everything that was going on. "Your sisters will be thrilled to have you with them in a few days, after the trial."

"Can I see them before?" Mateo looked at the shorter man with eyes shining with hope.

"You might not understand the risk of word getting out to Pomares that you're alive and kicking, but I for one would prefer to keep all of us breathing until this is over. My daughter has her fifteenth birthday in two weeks, and I want to enjoy it with her. God knows it's costing me everything we have." Mateo remembered the only fifteenth birthday party he'd been able to attend, for his oldest sister Lisbet. They'd invited half of Topes de Collantes, and his father had hired a photographer all the way from Trinidad to take pictures. He wondered what, if anything, they had been able to do for Heidi and Corina when they'd turned fifteen. He shook his head, knowing it was best not to think about things he could do nothing about.

"We might as well get going, then," Mateo said, as much to himself as the other man.

"You don't happen to have any coffee prepared, do you?"

Mateo laughed out loud, releasing his tension finally. "I have a thermos from this morning. There's enough for the three of us."

"Better bring a bag from the shed, then, 'cause you're not gonna like what the coffee tastes like where we're going." Mateo nodded in agreement, and turned toward the house to retrieve the thermos and three glasses.

"You know where they are. I'll pour us one for the road."

PART
TWENTY-TWO

Heidi returned to the house with Corina in tow, as was usual. They were inseparable. And when Juanito wasn't in school, they were the three musketeers, but Lisbet always told them they reminded her more of the three stooges. They had been racing the last block, as was their tradition. Heidi was thin and sleek, and could easily beat her sister who was getting to be more than a little overweight, besides the stunted growth of her legs, but she always tried to make it a tie.

The two girls almost fell onto the chairs at the small table, trying to catch their breath.

"You're too old to give your big sister a kiss when you come in, now?" Lisbet admonished them. Both girls dutifully stood up and kissed their sister on the cheek. With their mother gone, Lisbet was the closest they had to a mother, now, and she assumed the role with pride and dignity, doling out praise and punishment in equal portions, just as she did with her son. When the girls had caught their collective breath, she pointed them to the wooden sofa with the torn wicker backrests. The girls knew there was something coming whenever they were remanded to the sofa.

"Is something wrong, Lisbet?" Heidi reacted to the strange look on Lisbet's face, not able to tell at first glance if it was sadness or joy in her eyes.

"Far from wrong, actually. I have news."

Corina noticed the absence of Juanito, and a panic washed over her. "Is there something wrong with Juanito? Where is he? He should be here by now. It's nearly dark."

Lisbet waved her hand for Corina to stop talking long enough for her to explain.

"I asked Juanito to stay at Josefina's place for dinner tonight, so I could talk to the two of you alone."

It was Heidi's turn to fear the worst, and she tried to get Lisbet to allow her to interject. Lisbet silenced her, too, with a look.

"Before I tell you the surprise, I want you to try some of the new coffee that I received today." The girls shared a look like their sister had lost a marble while they were out. Meanwhile, Lisbet poured three tiny cups in the only ones with finger grips. The girls knew immediately there was something special in the air. These cups were reserved for guests, and there were no guests in the house. Corina took hers in two hands – she was the reason there weren't a full set of six complete cups. Heidi was the first to taste the coffee, and looked over the edge of the cup at her sister, watching for her reaction. She'd never tasted anything as wonderful in her life, and she could tell that Lisbet knew it, too. The smile on her sister's face told her as much.

The smile turned into a question mark. There was no money for buying the coffee in the dollar shops, reserved for diplomats and foreigners. And it surely wasn't the coffee from the monthly quota book. That tasted more like cereal than coffee, with so many other things blended in with the coffee.

"You might just be old enough to remember," Lisbet started. "Mother let you taste the last drops from her cup when you were a toddler."

The question didn't leave Heidi's expression. "This coffee is from our farm?"

Lisbet set her cup down on the counter, far enough from the edge so as not to slide off. "A man came today and gave us a bag of coffee, and said he was a friend of our brother."

"He knew Mateo?" Heidi was all ears.

"That's what I want to talk to you both about." She motioned for them to once again take their places on the sofa, and she sat on the edge of the matching chair, facing them. "He didn't know him before. He knows him now."

Heidi's hand began to shake, and she quickly handed off her cup to her older sister.

"But Mateo was killed in the accident." Her eyes filled with fresh tears, reliving the pain of the news they were given by Captain Jimenez only weeks before.

Corina slurped the last drops from her cup, and lost interest in the conversation at hand. She spied her rag doll on the bed, and Lisbet nodded her permission to go and play with it. At seventeen years old, she still had the mentality of a five-year-old. She wouldn't grasp what she was being told, anyway.

Lisbet went to the kitchen and brought back the bag of coffee, and the note she had found shortly after the men had left. "Does this look familiar to you?" she asked, pointing to the hand-drawn pocket watch on the package.

Heidi searched it for a few seconds. "Didn't our dad have a watch like that, once?"

"Not like that... exactly that watch, and it was your grandfather's before our dad's, and it was Mateo's until it was taken from him. That's how I knew Mateo was really alive, and I knew he would try to contact us if he was." She carefully unfolded the note.

Slowly, deliberately, Heidi looked from the note to her sister's tear-filled eyes. "Is... that... from Mateo?" Just saying his name caused her throat to swell and she could say no more.

"It's short, but let me read it to you." She filled her lungs with air, trying to find the courage to read out loud what she had done silently a dozen times before the girls returned.

Heidi felt the need to be closer to her sister at that moment, and threw her arms around Lisbet's waist, resting her head on her shoulder to read the note with her.

"'To my dearest sisters, first I want to tell you of my deep sorrow at not being there with all of you during the illness and passing of our cherished mother. My heart aches at the thought of you going through it alone, and of me not holding her hand as she passed. Second, the news of my death was a lie. I escaped and have been recovering with the help of a guardian angel, Paolito, who also lost a son in a prison camp like the ones I was in for so long. I remain a fugitive with no identification or means of surviving outside of this little farm. Until I can, I hope to help you in some small way by selling coffee that we roast here. For the moment I have nothing more to offer you than my undying love and the promise we will be together one day soon. Your loving brother, Mateo.'" Lisbet handed the note to Heidi, knowing how it had soothed her to feel something that her brother had held in his own hands.

"Lisbet," Heidi began, little more than a whisper, "Do you think I could have just a little more of Mateo's coffee?" Both of them crumbled into the other's arms and wept. Corina played quietly on the bed, unaware of the emotional event only a few feet away.

PART
TWENTY-THREE

Pomares was thankful that at least he was being held in a special area of the prison in Havana, removed from the general population. There were too many there that knew who he was, and enough whom he had personally sent to rot there. It had been so easy to accuse anyone who stood in his way of counter-revolutionary activities. No trial was necessary. A snap of his fingers, and signing a couple of official documents, and they were out of his sight, and his ascension up the ladder to a place he deserved could continue unimpeded.

He felt uncomfortable, though, out of his uniform, without his medals and stripes to show others the level of respect and admiration he merited. Once he had a chance to talk to Fidel and Raul in person, he'd get this all straightened out and get back to work. He'd asked for a private audience with them already, so it shouldn't take much longer. If the guard would come back soon, he'd find out when the meeting would be, and get some decent food and cold water.

Surely all of the things he'd done for the revolution would take precedence over a few minor indiscretions. Nobody's area of the country ran smoother than his. They would take that into consideration.

He'd convinced them to let him keep his pocket watch, after inspecting it closely. He loved the watch, and especially what it represented to him personally. He wound it and snapped it shut, fingering the embossed eagle with pride. Strength and power. He was the eagle.

PART
TWENTY-FOUR

Mateo left the shop feeling like a different person. They'd put him up in the Hotel Inglaterra, just a block from the beautiful Capitolio and the theatre with the angels on the corners. He loved Havana – it was supposed to be the best city in Latin America, and he didn't doubt it. The streets were alive with cars and buses and well-dressed people moving around like they had somewhere to go, or tables of old men playing dominos in the park in front of the hotel. When the water came out of the shower pipes steaming hot, he had jumped out and had taken five minutes to figure out how to adjust the temperature to luke-warm. All of his life, he'd taken his baths with a tub of warm water from the stove and a pitcher to throw it onto himself, and rationing of water was always of the utmost importance. Here, in the hotel, he took his time, gradually raising the temperature and using half of the sweet-smelling bar of soap to clean every part of himself. When he was sure he was clean, he rested his head on the back of his neck and just let the water drench him. He opened his mouth and filled it with the warm liquid, spitting it out again. He shaved in the shower with real shampoo and ran his hands over his smooth cheeks. It wasn't until he was interrupted by a sharp knock at the door that he finally relented and turned off the water. He couldn't help but think about his mother and sisters, and how they would love this experience. He decided that when he got back on his feet, he would invite his sisters to stay in the hotel, or better yet, a hotel with a swimming pool for Corina.

It was the shorter man, who had finally introduced himself as Arnaldo, who had cut his bath short, probably at the request of the hotel staff. They had an appointment to cut his hair and buy the clothes and shoes for the trial. Arnaldo handed him a bag that Mateo immediately opened, revealing a package of new underwear – three pairs. It was like Christmas and his birthday. Back at home, birthdays were a day to receive some sort of clothing, and a pair of new underwear when he was a boy was more precious than the plastic trucks and tractors in the storefronts in Trinidad. Arnaldo was Cuban, too, so he understood the expression on Mateo's face. Child-like. A wordless expression of thanks, and Mateo had to turn away, waving his hand to Arnaldo to wait while he dressed in the other room. Aside from Paolito, this was the first person who had shown him kindness, albeit because it was his job, but there was a genuinely good person in Arnaldo, too. He could tell. His partner, Rodolfo, was okay, but not quite the same.

He felt almost bald as they left the barber shop around the corner from the hotel. He couldn't stop running his hand through his cropped hair. The barber had even styled it and massaged a perfumed gel into it before he finished, and swung the revolving chair around to reveal the new Mateo.

He protested the cost of the pants and shirt and tie, but Arnaldo insisted it was approved right from the top, and they knew their debt to him was far larger than new clothes and two or three nights in a hotel. Mateo smiled to himself at the confirmation he would have another night at least in paradise, and planned his next shower already.

There was a storefront next to the hotel with a long front window, and Mateo made a point of using it to examine the stranger in his reflection. He was tall, but with Arnaldo beside him he looked like a giant, and he noticed the attention he received from passing women. He hadn't felt the affection of a women since… he blushed suddenly, realizing that he had never felt the affection of a woman, ever. He had erased that part of his being, locked up for more than ten years with stinking men, and having been ripped from his home so near his wedding night. He didn't like to think about Gladys anymore, as it always brought the pain of holding her dying father in his arms so long ago. Even though Mateo was still a relatively young man at thirty years old, he felt like that part of his life was long gone. When a very dark-skinned woman of about forty looked him up and down and made a sound like she was enjoying a piece of chicken, he felt the skin on the back of his neck warm. Arnaldo enjoyed the attention, even though it was second-hand, and made little comments to Mateo about how attractive the woman had been as they passed her and caught her looking back for a different view. Mateo was a strikingly handsome man, with his blond hair and thin physique. The new clothes were the final touch.

"Let's keep our minds on the trial tomorrow, and leave that for after." Arnaldo gave Mateo a friendly elbow to the ribs.

"That's a long way down my priority list right now," Mateo responded, fiddling with the collar of his shirt, and loosening the tie. It was his first time with anything that tight around his neck, and he didn't feel comfortable at all.

"Well, don't keep it too far down the list, Mateo. There're a whole lot of flowers in the garden, and somebody needs to tend to them." He gave Mateo a friendly shove he hadn't expected, and nearly collided with one of the flowers Arnaldo was talking about. She didn't seem to mind the close call, either.

He wondered again where Gladys might be at this very moment, and with whom, and how many little Gladyses were chasing her around her home. He was brought back to the present when they arrived at the hotel to drop off his old clothes and shoes before his meeting with the military prosecution team. They were going to explain the procedures and order of events of the following morning. Due to the security risk, they wanted everything to happen as quickly as possible. Sergeant Pomares had amassed a considerable following of capable soldiers. They were expecting some resistance, and Fidel had provided instructions to his top advisers to squash any before it began. Arnaldo hadn't bothered to mention that they were being shadowed by four undercover agents, on high alert for any undesired attention. Nothing, so far, according to their signals to Arnaldo.

In his room, Mateo laid out his own clothes and shoes, the way he had done as a young man at home. His mother always had a fresh shirt and pants pressed and his dress shoes spotless anytime he had a trip to Trinidad planned to sell coffee or buy supplies. It had been so long since he'd had a real change of clothes that it brought back suppressed memories of that happy time, and he felt his eyes water, thinking about his dear mother, and all of the things she had done for him and his sisters over the years.

He went into the bathroom and splashed water on his face, trying to bring himself back to the present. He had a mission to take care of, and the sooner it was over, the sooner he could be free to be with his sisters. Free, he knew, wasn't the right word anymore in Cuba. He had to at least attempt to believe Arnaldo that he was to be taken to his sisters after the results of the trial had been carried out, and from there they would be relocated to a suitable place, although not back to his ranch, anytime soon.

A brisk knock at his door signaled it was time to go.

PART
TWENTY-FIVE

Pomares whispered to the guard who tried to look inconspicuous as he pretended to tie his boot strap outside the private cell. It was difficult to hear, but Pomares was certain he got the gist of the instructions. He was to find out who had betrayed him, and get the information back to him before nightfall, because he needed to get to that person before the trial. The same guard, who as it turned out was related to one of Pomares' inner circle, had slipped the note into his cell with his breakfast, telling him what he'd learned from the briefing earlier – the sergeant was being charged with orchestrating the murder and cover-up of the prisoners being transported to Pinar del Rio. It was the final nail in an on-going investigation into his empire-building, as it had been labeled.

Pomares returned to his uncomfortable bunk and squeezed his knuckles into his closed eye sockets, trying to make his eyeballs contact the part of his brain that could tell him who had betrayed him for what had happened that day. He'd chosen each of the Special Forces men precisely because they'd demonstrated their loyalty to him time and time again. He knew the answer without knowing the details – Fidel was too smart and too well trained in the Russian KGB tactics to not have someone working secretly for him in every corner of every region. When he found out, he'd remove the bastard's tongue and send it to the commandant.

He opened his eyes, and waited for the bright bursts of light and color to subside from the pressure he'd been applying, until the unpainted ceiling with its single dull yellow bulb came into focus. There was no doubt as to the message he was being presented with this kind of treatment. He was officially an outsider – an enemy of the state. He had witnessed first-hand on three other occasions the punishment for crossing the line with the Castros. He felt a knot form in his stomach, remembering the way one of the men had cried like a baby and called out to his mother to save him, the hood thankfully hiding his face, but not the stain that ran down his leg at the sound of the military judge ordering the squad to take aim. It had been horrible, that one – an officer that Pomares had taken training with in Matanzas in the early years of the Revolution – strong, proud and capable. His legs had given out at the last instant, causing most of the shots to miss their intended target, and they'd needed to reload and fire again while he screamed in agony on the ground in his own blood and shit and piss.

He vowed to himself that he would not allow that to happen to him. He'd be more like the second man who he'd witnessed as he was executed. He refused the hood, telling them he wanted to look them in the eyes as they pulled the trigger. That guy had been tough. A mentor for Pomares to aspire to. He knew the trial was just a technicality. If it'd gotten this far, there was no defense he could raise that would reverse Fidel's decision. He'd been present on more than a few occasions when all those present had been contrary to the president's opinion, but it was not swayed in the least by dissent. Opposition needed to be crushed quickly and decisively. Cuba was not a democracy. Democracies were weak and flawed, he'd reminded them. Majorities could be equally badly informed and under-qualified to do the right thing. A leader who waited for consensus showed weakness and doubt, two things Fidel was incapable of displaying.

It was time to reflect on his accomplishments. His father never had a penny to his name, and his brothers worked in the cane fields to scratch out a living. He was the only one who had risen out of the dust and made something of himself. He had dined with Fidel and Che. He had the money in the account with his children's names attached, so they would have access to it if...

His wife had the apartment and another home that her mother had left her when she'd passed. She'd be fine, with the help of their married daughters. The mistress was another story, but she was young and pretty, and he knew she had another boyfriend besides him, anyway. She would have to be satisfied with all of the jewelry and gifts he'd bought her over the last couple of years. She could live for a year off of just that fat gold chain she'd insisted on. He suspected it was for the boyfriend right from the start. Women didn't wear chains that heavy. Oh well, he'd gotten what he wanted, and she got what she wanted, so no hard feelings either way.

The only thing he regretted was never having had a son. He loved his daughters, and they had given him a grandson each, but it wasn't the same. He had dreamed of seeing another Ruben Pomares grow up strong and powerful like himself.

His last act, though, he was sure, would be to ensure the bastard who ratted on him would die a slow and painful death. There were a couple of guys he knew who took enormous pleasure in their ability to cause excruciating pain. He'd make their day, he knew.

He had drifted off mentally ticking names from his list of close associates, trying to determine which one of them had turned on him, and why. His conscious mind blended into his unconscious one, and faces from his past and present appeared and disappeared randomly. He hadn't been asleep long, though, before the hands clasps his throat from behind once again, and he forced himself awake with a small squeal. His immediate reaction was to look around to see who might have seen or heard, until he realized where he was. He felt the urge to have a drink of rum. It was always there to help him forget the dreams. Even his bottles had abandoned him, now.

PART
TWENTY-SIX

There was a small press area inside of the military court, which had once been a home of some mafia character or other, forced to flee the country only days after the triumph of Fidel and his band of merry men. The area of the trial was what had once apparently been a magnificent foyer where extravagant parties must have taken place. The ten-foot diameter chandelier still hung from the ceiling some twenty feet in the air, and a balcony wrapped the entire area on the second story. The ornate carving of the marble of the railing would have cost more than most entire homes at the time. Though stripped of all of the furnishings from its day, and replaced with sober-looking benches and heavy wooden chairs and tables, the majesty of the home couldn't be masked. The marble on the floors still shone as always, and the thickness of the walls that could be seen in the window wells magnified the 'money-is-no-object' vulgarity of the structure. This kind of home was the poster child for Fidel's revolution, and his decision to turn them all into embassies, schools and other institutions was another reason for the reverence he received from the population.

The judge looked too old to have climbed the three steps up to his bench, and if not for the fact his Churchill-like chin seemed to have a rhythm all its own, swaying in a non-existent breeze, one might have thought2 he was a statue. His eyes seemed to be closed, until after what appeared to be an eternity, he lifted them from the document he had been reading carefully.

Pomares was escorted to his chair at the defendant's table, accompanied by his lawyer and a junior assistant. At the other table, a pair of soldiers in full uniform and medals stood at attention, waiting for permission to sit. The judge gave it to them with a small wave of his hand, gesturing for them to take their seats.

"Mr. Ruben Pomares," the judge began in an even voice. "I have read the list of charges against you. Do you understand the severity of what you have been charged with?"

His lawyer moved to stand up, but Pomares held him with an out-stretched arm. He stood and stared at the judge as though he were a junior officer. "First of all, I am Sergeant Ruben Pomares Alvarez, commander of the south central region of Cuba. Mr. Ruben Pomares was my father."

He was about to continue when the judge pounded his gavel on the oak block. "When you were accused of crimes against the Revolution of Cuba, you lost your privilege to refer to yourself as an officer of the Cuban government. Please be seated, and speak when you are requested to."

Pomares raised his shoulders higher, still, and looked the judge in his eyes. "The fact that I have been accused of many things does not make me guilty, until proven so in this court. Until that moment, I am Sergeant Ruben Pomares Alvarez, and I demand to be addressed as such."

The judge's face quivered just the slightest, as he held his desire to pass sentence before the trial had begun. Instead, he signaled to the two enormous bailiffs who framed his simple bench in contrast to the elaborate designs on the borders of the walls behind him. With hardly a nod from either of them, they proceeded to restrain Pomares to the arms of his chair with tight straps just at his elbows, forcing him to a seated position and severely inhibiting any movement. When Pomares stopped struggling, realizing he had no hope of escape, the judge quietly lifted a long black bandana-like object, twisted it a few times conspicuously, and laid it in front of him on the table for all to see. "I am going to assume that Mr. Pomares understands the charges against him."

Pomares tried to intimidate the judge with his unblinking stare, but apparently this wasn't the older man's first trial of a high-ranking official, and he was not in the least impressed by Pomares' attempt.

"I have read the statements of the accusing individuals, who have chosen to remain anonymous, and have been granted that request personally by the Commandant Fidel Castro Ruz. In their sworn statements, two soldiers independently presented identical accounts of the events that occurred on the 14th of September of this year. The deaths of three prisoners who had received unconditional pardons, each signed on that same day by the defendant, along with the execution-style shooting of the driver of the vehicle the prisoners were being transported in, were all under specific orders from Mr. Pomares. The fact the men had all been pardoned previous to their deaths makes the crime significantly more heinous, given they were all free men, and citizens of the Revolution of Cuba."

The judge paused briefly, long enough to catch the eyes of Pomares, ensuring he understood the error of the timing of the events. Had he executed the three men in prison, for the slightest hint of provocation, he might be receiving a medal for bravery now.

"Osvaldo Enrique Gomez Pineda, 46 years old – father of four children, grandfather of three, survived by his wife Elena; Angel Castillo Morales, 33 years old – married to Elissa, father of one girl; Antonio Torres Salazar, junior officer, driver for the prison, 24 years old, expecting his first child." The judge had spoken the words with no emotion – matter-of-factly, relying on the family connections to amplify the range of destruction.

Pomares looked at the space behind the judge, noticing how the cracks in the marble looked like the maps he had spread on the walls behind his desk in Trinidad. Some looked like rivers and tributaries. Others looked like roadways to unknown destinations. He heard the names of the men being read out loud by the judge, and subconsciously waited for the fourth one to be spoken out loud – the others were just collateral damage, something Fidel himself had used to justify dozens of actions taken over the years. When the judge stopped reading, his head cocked ever-so-slightly to the side, awaiting the moment of ignition when the can of gasoline was thrown onto the fire.

The roads and rivers lost their focus in the deafening silence where Mateo's name should have been read. Seconds were eternity. He looked the judge in the eye, willing him to read the name.

The judge set the paper onto the table in front of him, looking up from it and catching Pomares' stare. He pursed his lips and asked the accused with his eyes what he might possibly be waiting for.

Pomares felt like the judge was actually looking at the scar on his face that had been caused so many years ago when Mateo had first beaten him up. Did the judge know where he'd received the scar? Did everyone know? Read the damn name and get this circus over with.

From a side door, to the left of the judge, a tall man in a suit was escorted into the courtroom and shown to the witness box. It was only when the man turned his face to look directly at him that Pomares realized it was Mateo himself, so different with the haircut and clean, pressed suit. There was a silence in the room while the two men locked their eyes on one another, and Pomares' bottom jaw unconsciously separated from the top one. How…

"Mateo Cardenas Ramos, can you identify the accused as the person who ordered your incarceration for more than ten years?" The judge brought the whispers from the press behind Pomares to a stop with a wave of his gavel before he addressed Mateo.

"I can, Sir. The man sitting in front of me, Ruben Pomares." Mateo trembled as he spoke, but not from fear. The years of prison, his mother's death, so many others still there, rotting. He hated being so close to the man without throttling the life from him.

"And do you have reason to believe the accused was behind the killing of your fellow prisoners and the driver of the Jeep in September?"

"Yes, Sir. I overhead one of the soldiers telling another that Pomares would be upset that they didn't have my corpse to bring back as proof of my death."

The defense attorney stood to object, but the judge overruled him. Normal rules definitely did not apply in a trial called for directly by Fidel Castro.

Pomares couldn't help remembering how he had screamed at the two soldiers for nearly ten minutes that evening, when they told him they didn't bring back Mateo's body because it was too far down the ditch to retrieve, and they were interrupted by the vehicles. He'd sent them away for a month without pay. Useless liars. He should never have sent them. He should have gone himself.

His hands instinctively clenched and unclenched, trying to regain control so he could reach for his sidearm and finish what he'd started so many years ago. He couldn't move them more than an inch, and there was no gun to reach for in his prison garb. How he wished he could have at least been dressed in his uniform with all of his medals and stripes.

Mateo choked on his anger and emotion at being in front of the man he had lost so much to over so many years. The judge nodded to the bailiff to escort Mateo out through the same side door.

"Thank you Mister Cardenas. You can step down, but be available should we require anything further."

Mateo was relieved to get off of the stand, and more relieved to get Pomares out of his sight. But he knew there was a lot more he wanted to say to him, and hoped he'd have a chance before it was all over.

PART
TWENTY-SEVEN

Paolito arrived to an empty house, which didn't surprise him. Mateo seldom spent any time in the house if he wasn't sleeping or eating. When he got no response from the work shop, though, the few hairs he had left began to bristle on the back of his neck. He noticed the mule still had some hay and oats and water, so he hadn't been gone for more than a day. The thing was, Mateo had nowhere to go. Paolito knew he wouldn't have left the farm without waiting to hear what had happened with his sisters, and without telling him where and why. Julio helped him search the place, and it was during that time they noticed all of the improvements – fences mended, fresh paint still drying on the walls of the shop and house, plumbing repairs.

The clues didn't help Paolito to conclude what might have been the reason for Mateo's absence. He could have done all of this out of gratitude before leaving, or he might have done them simply because they needed doing, and it had been easier to do when Paolito was absent.

They didn't have time to come up with additional scenarios before they saw the car approaching from down the lane. Paolito recognized it as the same one the inspectors had come in earlier.

The taller man, Rodolfo, had come to the farm as soon as he received word that Paolito and Julio were near. There had been a car parked near the entrance to their property, with its hood raised and an agent posing as a mechanic working under the hood, to be sure there had been no undesired visitors while they were away. He had already received communication from Arnaldo that there had been no incidents in Havana, and that Mateo had been prepped for the short trial. It was just a formality, really. The trial was over and the verdict decided the moment Mateo appeared before Pomares, alive and well.

Rodolfo spent the afternoon explaining to Paolito what had happened, assuring him there would be no repercussions for harboring a fugitive, because the truth was he had been harboring a free man. He explained also that Mateo had made it clear that his first stop after completing his duty was Pinar del Rio, where his sisters would be waiting in a secure area. Mateo would make his decision of when to come back to Paolito's farm after the sentence was carried out.

Paolito had to sit down to take it all in. In one way, he was extremely happy for Mateo, having been exonerated from his status as a fugitive, and he would soon be reunited with his sisters. On the other hand, though, he felt like he was losing another son, and the ranch was going to be a very lonely place again. He had just gotten accustomed to his son not being there when Mateo came along. Now he had to get used to seeing that bedroom door closed once again.

Paolito found himself wandering from the house to the shed where the mule even looked sad to him. He ran his hand over the newly-repaired beam that Mateo had installed while he had been gone. He saw how Mateo had actually made a proper joint where he had originally held it together with twisted wire and a prayer, as his wife had always chided him. Mateo had prepared a proper manger so the hay wouldn't fall and get mixed with the dirty straw. It was something that his own son had planned and never got the chance to do.

In the coffee workshop, Mateo noticed fresh paint, freshly-swept floors and dozens more bags of coffee hand-drawn and ready for filling. He smiled when he saw the funnel system Mateo had fashioned from an old tin can. It was held in place with two upright pieces of wood so that one person could easily manipulate the bags and fill them without help. He was almost surprised not to see a functioning conveyor belt.

He wanted to think Mateo had done all of this to make his own life easier, but he knew all too well that Mateo had been doing it for his benefit. A part of him wanted to just go and sit in his arm chair until he passed to the next life, but a far bigger part of him wanted to honor his son and Mateo and make sure their sacrifices weren't in vain.

He studied the wooden structure with the tin funnel for a minute, and began to understand the logic. A sack of ground coffee sat near the work bench, and he saw that if he placed it on the right side, it would be at the correct angle to feed the powder into the funnel. There was a handle at the top of the funnel that would allow coffee to be fed into the bag, and when it was full, he could pull the handle and the top of the can would slide into place, stopping the flow.

He calculated that there were enough bags in the pile to package two or three sacks of coffee. He eyed the heavy sack, wishing Mateo was there to lift it for him. That was when he noticed the old block and tackle fixed to the beam above the filling device. A rope hung from it, with a strap that could be wrapped around the sack. He shook his head, and swatted a fly from the back of his neck. A gecko stared at him from the next beam, seeming to ask him what other excuse he had for not getting to work. He pulled the old hat off his head and hung it on a nail behind him. He wrapped the straps around the sack of grounds, and marveled at how easy it was to lift it into place. Mateo hadn't abandoned him after all. He was there helping him right at that moment.

Sack in place, he clicked the light that Mateo had fixed near the base of the funnel, and reached for the first bag.

PART
TWENTY-EIGHT

Arnaldo and Mateo had walked from the Inglaterra to the malecon and turned west. An early-morning fisherman held up his ample catch to them as they passed, in case they were looking for a breakfast feast. A pair of young lovers couldn't contain their passion, even as the pair of men passed by them. A dozen seagulls quarreled about something as they swung overhead on their way back to the harbor. The castle on the other side looked foreboding as it guarded the entrance to the city by ship.

Even though Mateo had no previous experience in Havana, he was surprised at the number of military vehicles that passed them as they walked. All of them seemed to be of Russian heritage – big, square, strong and with no regard for emissions, belching black smoke as they prowled their new territory. There were Ladas and other Russian cars on the street, too. Mateo realized that in the time he'd been in prison, Cuba had converted into something he had never imagined. He'd only heard smatterings of what had happened during the missile crisis and Bay of Pigs invasion. News didn't find its way into the prison camps.

Across the street he spied an ice cream shop, and saw a woman in a bright dress emerge from the shop with two young children, happily working at keeping their cones from leaking in the warm air. He was buoyed by this image. It reminded him of the first flowers in spring. There was always something pretty to remind him that all was not bleak and dreary.

Arnaldo reminded him that they needed to get back to the courtroom for the verdict, so they crossed at the stop light at the corner of Infanta, looking up at the National Hotel, one of the city's finest. There was an incline in the street for a few blocks before they would turn east toward the Capitolio and the hotel. The woman with the pretty dress made eye contact with Mateo as they passed, and he was able to see her with more detail. She looked like a movie star from the films he had once seen in the cinema in Trinidad. Even though she had an ice cream cone in her hand, her lips remained cherry red from her lipstick, and her hair had been curled and styled to highlight her cheekbones and her eyes had a greenish tint that he thought were possibly the prettiest he had ever seen in his life. He tried not to stare as they passed, but it was impossible. Instead of being angry, though, she gave him a broad smile with perfect white teeth, and then turned her attention to her youngest child, whose ice cream was running down his arm.

In that instant, Mateo remembered that he was a man, and he wanted – no, he needed, a woman in his life. One like that one would do just fine, he smiled to himself. Arnaldo had noticed the exchange, as he, too, had appreciated the beautiful woman.

"Doesn't cost anything to dream," he chided Mateo. "A handsome man like you could find a dozen like her."

"There aren't two like her on this earth," Mateo combatted. "But I'd settle for her ugliest sister in a heartbeat." The two laughed at Mateo's sudden change in humor.

The incline of the street seemed to disappear, as the two men picked up their pace. A parrot on a balcony of a second-story apartment called to them with language meant for a brothel, and Mateo laughed and clapped Arnaldo on the back. "I'm pretty sure she was talking to you, Arnaldo, because I'm a country gentleman."

"You weren't thinking about the farm a few minutes back when you passed by Greta Garbo with her ice cream."

"Son of a gun, that parrot is a mind-reader!" They had to stop walking, they laughed so hard.

By the time they got to the hotel it was time to change clothes and go straight to the courtroom. Arnaldo's suggestion of going for a walk had served its purpose. There hadn't been time to think about the trial.

Mateo had his clothes laid out on the bed, ready for when he got back. He would take a quick shower, this time, and meet Arnaldo in the lobby. He couldn't help but think about the woman with the ice cream. There had been something so special in her eyes, and the two young children with her. Family. That was it.

He was still pulling the shirt over his head as he entered the bathroom, and might have not seen it had he turned his head to the left and not to the right as he reached into the shower to open the hot water tap. There, in the deep sink, was a gigantic dead rat. At the first instant, Mateo was repulsed by the hotel cleanliness, until his peripheral vision caught the one-word message written with soap on the mirror. 'Die', with an arrow pointing down toward the animal. Mateo stumbled out of the bathroom, water still running in the shower. His next thought was that someone might still be in the room, so he made for the door.

He knew Arnaldo was in the room next to his, so he pounded on the door, knowing he was probably showering, himself. Arnaldo opened the door, still wet, with a towel wrapped around his waist. The look on Mateo's face was all he needed to bring him to high alert, and his first reaction was to find his gun.

Mateo calmed him with a raised hand. "It was just a message for me." He said, looking back toward his own room. Just being out of the room made him feel better, and having Arnaldo to confirm what he had seen made him calm.

Now, though, his emotions transformed from calm to furious. Pomares was behind this, too. The man could not accept defeat, and could not let him live a peaceful life. To think, he chided himself, he had actually felt sorry for the man he had confronted the afternoon before in the courtroom, knowing that the punishment for treason in Cuba was a firing squad. He had quietly wished his arch enemy would suffer for as many years as he had in a prison somewhere, but not anymore. His life, and those of his sisters, would never be safe from threats and violence until Pomares was dead. Now he couldn't wait to stare him down as the sentence was read.

PART
TWENTY-NINE

Pomares was pleased the guard had found a way to get the message to Mateo. He'd earned the money he'd gotten to him through another contact. If he was going to suffer, then Mateo would suffer doubly. He was still incensed that he'd been lied to about the events of the day on the highway, when all of the prisoners and the driver were supposed to have been disposed of. The only one he really cared about eliminating had been the one who'd escaped. Typical, he thought to himself. The bastard always seemed to come out on top. He fingered the scar on his face, his constant reminder of the day that turned him toward his career path. Why bring a bat when you could bring a battalion?

His wife would miss him. Mostly because of habit than anything else. She'd been a good woman. A good mother to the children who had hardly spoken a word to him in years. She'd keep herself busy with the grandchildren and her infernal crocheting. He sometimes worried they would be trapped under a mountain of blouses and dresses and baby booties. She never moved without her ball of twine and crochet needle. He'd woken her up on dozens of occasions in front of a white screen on the television, with a half-finished shawl or some other thing hanging from her rocking chair.

He tried to remember when he'd been replaced by her crochet hook as the most important thing in her life. The fact he couldn't remember only served to confirm that it had probably been him and not her who had been the catalyst of that transition. When had his daily bottle of rum replaced her?

Just the thought of rum gave him a moment of despair. Pavlov's dog salivated at the ringing of a bell, and he salivated at the thought of uncapping a bottle of good rum. He'd always wanted a dog, he thought to himself. He hated the old cat his wife had rescued and insisted on allowing all over the furniture. He wouldn't miss that thing.

The guard came by again, this time to tell him it was time to go to the court for the reading of the verdict. More like the sentence. He and everybody else knew the verdict the day he'd been charged. His mind found its way to Camilo Cienfuegos, and how he'd disappeared so soon after crossing the Castro brothers in public. Unlikely any school kids would be singing for him and tossing flowers into any rivers, though.

He had been sitting on the edge of the bed when the guard reminded him it was time to go, and in the moment that he stood, he felt his stomach rebel against him, and rushed to the cracked and yellowed toilet, where he emptied his bowels and vomited into the little garbage bin at the same time. Thankfully he found enough water in the tap to wash his face and brush his teeth with the last morsel of bitter paste.

PART THIRTY

Heidi shook Corina awake. She'd already been up for more than an hour, splashing water onto the front pad of cement outside. She wanted everything to be perfect, and Corina needed to help, too. Her only task was to make the two beds – the one she and her sister shared, and the bigger one that Lisbet and Juanito slept in in the only bedroom. Heidi had spent the night tossing and turning, deciding which of her three dresses would look best for the homecoming celebration.

Captain Jimenez himself had given them the news the day before that their brother Mateo was coming to Pinar del Rio in the afternoon, and that permission had been granted for a celebration. Lisbet had worried herself sick that there was nothing to celebrate with, until she opened the door to find an army of neighbors, arms filled with their offerings – two chickens from one, a half dozen sweet potatoes from another, rice, beans, onions and garlic. Her eyes watered at the sight of so many people coming together for her and her family. Plans were made for who would be in charge of the rice and beans, who would roast the chickens and they decided to make a big community stew over a fire in the common area between the four apartments in their corner of the small city. Antonio in building seven had the big caldron they'd used for the New Years party last year. The men got busy finding enough bottles of rum that had been squirrelled away for just such an occasion.

News of Mateo's miraculous return from the dead had spread throughout the entire region, and anyone who had friends or family who had shared time with him in the prisons touted him as a hero. He was like a soldier who had returned from a war after having been pronounced dead. Everyone wanted to be a part of the celebration.

Corina had her own plans for her brother's return. She quickly made the two beds, and asked her sister for approval before taking out the only pair of scissors they owned, and held up the magazine they'd all memorized over the years. It had been the only thing in color they owned. Lisbet smiled at her baby sister, with her pleading eyes and enthusiastic grin.

"Go ahead," she said, running her hands through Corina's curly black hair. "Just clean up the mess afterwards."

Corina squealed in delight as she raced to the table with her magazine and a little bottle of glue, and cut each page into inch-wide strips, to form into colorful chains, as she and her friends had done at the school where she spent her days.

Lisbet knew it would keep her occupied and give her and Heidi and Juanito more time for all of the things they needed to do. She'd already sent Juanito to the store with most of her savings to buy up all of the powdered mix to make drinks for the children. She'd gone personally to ask Alexandra, the young teacher, if she would be willing to bring her record player and records for the party. Everything in Cuba was precious, and it was a risk to take anything of value out of one's home. Alexandra agreed without hesitation, and told her she had already made plans to be there. She confirmed it was alright to bring along her daughter. She was four years old. Lisbet had an idea. "Does your daughter like to cut and glue paper chains, by any chance?"

Within fifteen minutes Corina had a helper for her mega project. Alexandra carefully unpacked the record player and connected it with a long extension cord so that the speakers faced the courtyard. She explained to Lisbet that it had been the pride and joy of her late husband, who had died from a heart condition two years earlier. He'd been a musician, and listened to his records every night until his death. She told her she hadn't been able to listen to music for more than a year, but now it was her therapy. Every song was a memory of better times.

Heidi was in a flutter, racing from room to room, looking for some hair brush or other. For her, this was a beauty pageant. Something inside her told her that she needed to be the prettiest girl in Cuba

for her big brother when he arrived. Maybe the fact
the handsome young Russian soldier she'd been
talking to the weekend before would probably show
up to the party had something to do with it, too.
Lisbet just shook her head and pointed Heidi in the
direction of whatever latest lost items she needed.
She passed the mirror in the hallway between the
bedroom and bathroom, and realized she should
take a few minutes to think about her appearance,
too. She looked more like her late mother than she
wanted to admit.

PART
THIRTY-ONE

The hotel staff quickly disposed of the evidence
in Mateo's room, and cleaned the mirror. Arnaldo
exchanged harsh words with the staff, who all
claimed amnesia when questioned about who might
have entered and left the hotel in the time they had
been out. Arnaldo knew that the most likely culprit
was an actual staff member themselves, and there
was little point in interrogating each of them
separately. He chose to call for additional plain-
clothed backup for their short trip to the courtroom,
and for increased vigilance there, as well.

Rodolfo had returned from Paolito's ranch, and would be another bookend with Arnaldo on the trip. The damage had been done. Mateo had made his appearance the day before, proving Pomares' guilt without any doubt. All that was left was the sentencing and carrying out of the sentence. Fidel had insisted there be no delay in either.

Mateo did his best to forget about the rat and the threat. He'd lived through a lot worse in prison and had come out the other side. Pomares was acting out of desperation, now, and he focused on getting it over with so he could be driven to Pinar del Rio as promised. He tried to imagine his sisters and nephew as they would be now. The older girls were easy – he knew them as women. It was Corina and Juanito he had the most trouble imagining. She would be nearly eighteen, now, and Juanito would be a young man of nearly twelve years old. He regretted not having anything to be able to bring all of them as gifts, but he would worry about that later.

They arrived without incident at the courtroom less than ten minutes later. Word had begun to spread about the military leader having been arrested, and there were enough people who craved the excitement that a crowd had gathered at the entrance. Arnaldo and Rodolfo sandwiched Mateo between them as they pushed their way through, ever vigilant of any threat. Someone shouted for Mateo to make a statement, but Arnaldo silenced the reporter with his raised hand, and signaled to the guard at the door to open it and not let anyone else pass.

Inside there was tranquility once again, and they found their way to the same room they had been in the afternoon before. Mateo took his place directly behind where the defendant would sit. He wanted to be close enough to look into his eyes when he was sentenced.

They didn't need to wait for long. Only minutes after their arrival, the door at the back of the chamber that led to the holding cells opened and two large uniformed soldiers entered and framed the doorway. Next came two additional soldiers, then Pomares with his hands cuffed behind his back, once again in his green uniform, but stripped of all medals and stripes. Behind him were two more guards, including the one who had provided him the information. He tried unsuccessfully to keep from glancing at Mateo with suspicion. He'd made some nice extra money over the past two days, and wouldn't mind at least one more payoff.

Mateo's attention was focused exclusively on Pomares, who returned the favor. Pomares tried his best to smirk, but it came out wrong. "Did you get my message?" he called out to Mateo, before he was silenced by the guard behind him.

"Pity you couldn't bring it to me yourself," Mateo rebuffed him. "I see you don't have your bat or your gun with you this time."

Pomares wanted to respond, but he was yanked into submission by the guard, and shoved roughly into his waiting seat. He was faced forward, and had his wrists once again strapped to the arm-rests.

Mateo seethed with anger. His saw his own hands forming fists and felt the blood pounding in the veins of his neck. He made a motion like he might get to his feet, and felt two sets of hands confine him to his seat. Rodolfo and Arnaldo both shook their heads at him to control his anger for just awhile longer.

The doors to the judge's chambers opened inward, and he waited until everyone but Pomares was standing before he hurried to his seat on the stage. He pounded his gavel three times, and motioned for everyone to be seated.

"As this is not a regular trial, but a military one, we will proceed without all of the ceremony and circumstance. I have the verdict in my hands. I will read it, and the defendant will have an opportunity to respond."

Pomares looked to his left, where the legal counsel sat in silence. He wanted him to intervene on his behalf, give him time to defend himself. When he made a comment to the lawyer, he was immediately silenced by the judge.

"Mr. Ruben Pomares Alvarez, EX officer of the military of the Revolutionary Government of Cuba, you have been tried in this military courtroom, and have been found guilty of treason against your country."

There was an audible gasp from Pomares, who hadn't expected the judge to act so quickly.

"The matter has been discussed with our Commandant Fidel Castro Ruz, and he has recommended death by firing squad, to be carried out this afternoon in the Plaza of the Revolution."

Pomares' chin dropped to his neck, and his hands gripped the hand-rests like he was holding onto them to keep from falling. Knowing what the outcome would be, and hearing it with his own ears were two different things entirely.

Even Mateo was surprised things had happened so quickly. There hadn't been time to enjoy Pomares' discomfort. He'd hoped for much more.

"Mr. Pomares, you have an opportunity to speak on your own behalf. Make it brief." The judge seemed as though he had a pressing appointment he needed to get to.

"May I be allowed to stand?" Pomares asked, quietly. He'd lost his authoritative sergeant's voice somewhere along the way.

The judge nodded to the guards to release Pomares' arms so that he could stand. One remained on either side of his chair, in case he tried to run.

"Your honor, I have served my country faithfully for fifteen years. If it is my fate to die for it, then I accept. I ask only that I be allowed to wear my uniform when I do so." He looked to the judge for any sign of acknowledgement.

"Request granted. You will wear your uniform, void of any medals or decoration." The judge snapped his gavel again, to declare what he said to be final. "Anything else, Mr. Pomares? Time is of the essence."

"I regret that I won't have time to say good-bye to my wife and daughters." Pomares swallowed to keep from crying.

"Your wife and daughters have been notified, and have chosen not to be here in Havana."

Pomares wiped at his eyes. He turned to see Mateo standing behind him, still glaring.

"Your son won't be there, either," Mateo whispered, loud enough for Pomares to hear him. "And don't worry, he doesn't have your last name."

Pomares turned completely around to look at Mateo, to confirm what he was saying with his eyes. Mateo stared into his eyes, and nodded his head in the affirmative.

"Don't worry, we'll take good care of him, as long as no harm comes to my sisters."

Mateo let it sink in. If Pomares had any plans to send anyone to avenge his death where it would hurt Mateo the most, he would be putting the only son he had at risk.

"It's not true." Pomares pleaded with Mateo to confirm it was a lie, but he had always suspected, especially the way Lisbet had hated him so much.

"That will be all, then," the judge declared, pounding his gavel for the final time, with renewed enthusiasm. "The defendant will be transported to the Plaza of the Revolution immediately to carry out his sentence."

Pomares found the attention of the guard who had been his informant, and shook his head slightly but clearly from side to side. The plan was off. He stared at the guard for a long moment, making sure he was clear. There would be no more money for the guard.

PART
THIRTY-TWO

News travelled quickly in Cuba by word of mouth. Gossip was the favorite pastime of most Cubans over the age of thirty, and a firing squad for a high-ranking military official made its way from one end of the island to the other like wild-fire. In Pinar del Rio, where everyone was related by a single phenomenon – a family member in a political prison somewhere on the island, people couldn't wait to connect him to their loved-ones. Maybe there'd be amnesty for some of them. Lisbet heard from a neighbor that the officer to be executed was none other than Ruben Pomares, from Topes de Collantes. Of course no one knew it was the biological father of her only child they were talking about, and she certainly wasn't going to tell anyone. She excused herself quickly when she heard the news, and closed herself into the bathroom, since it was the only room with a lock on the door. She had only just clicked the lock on the door when her emotional bubble burst, and she let out a guttural sound, followed by uncontrollable bouts of shoulder-shaking fits. She tried at first to stop herself from crying, to pull herself together, but it was too much for her to hold in. She had internalized the rape and the horrible things he'd said when he'd forced himself on her that night in the barn. He'd left her there, beaten and bleeding and naked, and actually spit on her before he left, muttering that Mateo couldn't defend them every time.

She had prayed for him to receive justice, even wished for his death. Now that it was coming true, she thought about Juanito. He had no idea who his father was, and was just getting to the age when he'd started to ask her. She'd made excuses why he didn't want to know, and even thought about making up a story that would throw him off the trail. He'd never had a father, other than Mateo, and had grown up in a loving home with his grandmother and his aunts. She didn't know why she felt sorry, then, that such a monster as Ruben Pomares was going to receive the punishment he so deserved.

Maybe, after this, she could even feel differently about herself, and not feel guilty and dirty every time a man looked at her.

PART
THIRTY-THREE

Somebody mentioned that Fidel Castro himself was watching the square from an undisclosed window in the tower. The square had been cleared of the throngs of people who liked to walk with their children where Fidel had delivered his famous speech when they arrived triumphantly in Havana. This was where the white dove had flown down and perched on his shoulder while he screamed his rally cry to the masses, some of whom dropped to their knees as though they were witnessing a divine moment in history. Every three meters, all around the circumference of the square, a soldier stood at attention, facing forward. Toward the rear of the square, six soldiers stood with rifles resting beside them, ten meters from the concrete wall that would be the backdrop for the execution.

The ribbon of soldiers opened enough to allow two highly-armored vehicles to pass through. They stopped only meters from the group of soldiers, and quickly escorted Pomares to his place directly in front of the shooters. He was flanked by four large soldiers on either side, one of whom carried a black hood in his hand.

From the other vehicle emerged the same judge, this time in full military dress, dripping with medals. He stood at attention, saluted the tower where he knew Fidel to be, and marched to the area in front of Pomares.

Mateo, Arnaldo and Rodolfo had been instructed to remain in the vehicle for security reasons, but still had a front-row seat for the performance. The same vehicle would take Mateo to Pinar del Rio, some three hours away, as soon as the deed was carried out.

"Mr. Ruben Pomares Alvarez, you have been tried and convicted of treason against the Revolutionary Government of Cuba, and sentenced to be executed by firing squad."

The judge signaled for the soldier to place the hood over his head, but Pomares waved him off. He stared at the judge in defiance, calling upon any courage he might have been able to summon. He looked from the judge to the vehicle he knew Mateo to be in, searching for a glimpse.

Against significant protests from Arnaldo and Rodolfo, Mateo forced his way out of the vehicle, showing the two men the enormous power he had. He waved off the advances of the guards outside of the vehicle, and made his way to beside the judge, close enough to see Pomares' face and eyes clearly. He wanted his face to be the last thing Pomares saw.

There was a flash of light from the tower, a signal to the firing squad to take their positions, and the officer next to them stepped forward to provide the instructions.

"Ready!" he hollered to them over the noise from the crowd outside of the ring of soldiers. The six soldiers picked up their rifles in unison, and took a single step to the side with their left feet, positioning their bodies. Mateo tensed along with them.

"Aim!" They shouldered their rifles, tilting their heads to take aim. Pomares sucked in as much air as he could hold, determined to keep his gaze fixed on Mateo. He felt his bladder give out, and felt the warm liquid run down his inner thigh. His eyes filled with tears. Mateo held his stare.

"Fire!" Six rifles exploded in the same instant. Five of them held bullets, and one a blank. It was the general way of releasing the executioners from the psychological guilt. They could all believe their gun had been the one with the blanks. Pomares dropped to his knees immediately, having braced himself as best he could. He had definitely died with the dignity he'd hoped for, under the circumstances. His lifeless body dropped to the left, and crumbled face down onto the concrete. The six soldiers were ushered from the square immediately, while a doctor was sent to declare the obvious.

"The will of the Revolution of Cuba has been carried out," declared the judge. He signaled to the soldiers on either side of Pomares to quickly remove the body.

Mateo found his way out of the shock of the moment, thankful to feel Arnaldo's hand on his shoulder, a step behind him. He didn't know why he was crying, but he couldn't contain himself.

The eight strong soldiers unfolded a black tarp that they planned to use to cover the body and carry it to the military truck. Mateo spoke quietly to the judge, who nodded his head.

"Turn him over," Mateo instructed the soldiers, who looked at him questioningly. "Turn him over," he repeated. This time, two soldiers looked to their superior, who nodded for them to go ahead, and they lifted Pomares by the shoulders enough so that they could lay him face-up.

Mateo walked purposefully toward the dead man, and when he was close enough, he reached into the pocket of the prisoner coverall, and grabbed the watch he knew Pomares would be carrying. He ripped the cloth where it had been attached, and turned toward the waiting vehicle, saying a silent thank you to the judge as he passed.

EPILOGUE

Mateo shuffled down the outside hallway of the house, carrying a small bag of rice and beans and coffee and salt. It had been months since the quota had been worth anything. Still, he had his group of families to visit, and aside from the inevitable cup of coffee, most of them provided him with a dollar or two for his trouble, and those few dollars a week kept some food on the table. His dear wife, Alexandra, had long-since forgotten who he was, or even who her own grown daughter and grandchildren were. She mostly just sat in the rocking chair and mumbled to herself. Somehow, though, if someone played the right piece of music, her face brightened and there was a glimpse of the pretty young teacher she had been when they'd met at the homecoming party back in Pinar del Rio.

A tourist named Keith had given him a nice folding cart that he used to transport the food to the different families in his route. Since it was his birthday, he'd accepted the cold beer. They'd made it a tradition over the years. Married to one of Mateo's regular clients, Keith and his wife had traded the little house around the corner from his place for this bigger one halfway across town. This year there'd been a ten dollar bill stuffed into his when he'd offered his hand after the beer. There'd be meat on the table tonight for his eighty-ninth birthday celebration.

Keith had made it known he wanted to hear Mateo's story, and plans had been made to sit down one day over a couple of beers.

The day never came, because Mateo felt a shooting pain in his chest a few weeks later, while standing in the line for potatoes for the quota. He'd heard somebody complain about the old man being too slow, and why did he need to pick up so many people's quotas. Couldn't they get their own? He had sat on the step of a nearby home with his hand on the wheeled cart to protect the potatoes until his granddaughter, well, technically his step-granddaughter, found a bicycle taxi to take him to the hospital. They were only a few blocks from the hospital, passing by the tourist's house, when Mateo closed his eyes for the last time.

Keith made it back to Trinidad in time to pay his respects to the family. Alexandra rocked in her rocking chair that had been brought to the funeral parlor for her. She smiled to herself and seemed to be swaying to a tune in her head. Her daughter and grandchildren made their rounds, thanking everyone for their respect. They had done a good job of preparing Mateo for the open casket wake, except that someone had taken the initiative to trim his long eye brows, making him look completely different. His granddaughter Briana had insisted that they grant him his final wish, to be buried with his cherished pocket watch, which she had personally wound the morning of the wake.

The tourist asked permission of Briana, and placed an ice-cold beer into the casket. He had gone across the street and purchased two beers for the occasion, drinking the second one and raising it in a toast to his cherished friend.

There were only a few close friends besides the family who made their way from the funeral parlor to the cemetery near the road that led to La Boca, the ocean-side community nearest to Trinidad. It was a hot day, and only the deceased and his immediate family rode in the funeral coach. From the entrance, the men of the family, along with Keith, carried the casket to the family plot, where it was gently lowered into place with the help of the two employees. They had their buckets of cement and water waiting nearby so that when the last of the family had gone, they would seal it against the elements. Keith and Briana were the last to leave. She folded herself into his shoulder as he guided her to the entrance.

Two years later, as was the tradition, family members would exhume the casket to gather the bones of their loved one, and place them into a smaller container, leaving the space available for the next to go.

Briana had insisted she could do it alone, but Keith would have nothing of it. He would help her with this emotional and difficult task. Mateo deserved it. It was the first time he'd ever been near such a thing, and it turned his stomach at the very idea. But he couldn't leave it to Briana, and none of the other members of the family had volunteered. He'd contracted a local carpenter to prepare a beautifully-decorated box for the bones to be kept in. It looked like a very large cigar humidor, and had been made of black oak and cedar. He'd asked the artisan to try to replicate the eagle pattern on the coffee packages he'd kept as a memento ever since he heard that Mateo had been a part of the brand so many years earlier.

Briana suggested that both of them carry out the task of gathering the bones and placing them into the box. Even though he was claustrophobic, Keith agreed, and when the workers slid the concrete cover off and leaned it against the side of the structure, he helped her down to where she could stand beside the coffin. He handed her the hammer he had brought to open the wooden lid, and slid down on the opposite side. They shared a look that confirmed both were taken aback by the closeness and the foul smell, and the tourist handed her a pair of gloves and a white dust mask, and pulled on his own. He nodded his intention to her and pounded the forks of the hammer between the layers of wood, feeling how easily it penetrated the rotting material. There was a puff of fine dust as the top of the casket broke in half, disintegrating. He pulled the remainder off and tossed the crumbling pieces of wood to one side, revealing what he had secretly hoped he could have avoided: his friend of more than fifteen years, turned into dust and bones and hair and fingernails. He had known about the phenomena of things that continued to grow after death, and saw the twisted, yellowed fingernails, but he couldn't get over the fact that the signature Schnauzer eyebrows had grown back to the way they had been before. He smiled at the image, thinking about how Mateo's old-man eyebrows had been a subject of friendly ribbing over the years. He also smiled when he saw the empty beer bottle. The cap had rusted off, so the beer would have drained out on its own, or been consumed by the worms and other bugs that aided with the decomposition, but Keith liked to think Mateo had enjoyed it while it had still been cold.

Briana had been intent on something elsewhere, so she didn't see what the tourist was smiling about until he pointed to them, and gestured about how long they were again. She nodded, and returned to what she had been busy at earlier. She was painstakingly gathering all of the separate bones from his feet, careful not to miss any. They had forgotten the advice to put wool socks on the hands and the feet, to keep the bones from dispersing. Briana worked her way up from the feet, while Keith gently laid the skull into the box, and cradled the separate sections of his spinal column and ribs. He had been a big man, and his bones were thick and strong, even after so much time had passed.

The tourist was placing the last of Mateo's ribs into the box, and mentally calculating if it was going to be big enough, when Briana shrieked and pointed for him to help her out. There was an urgency to her frantic pointing and screaming that caused the tourist to almost throw her out of the grave before finding his own way.

"What time is it? What time is it?" Briana seemed to have lost her mind, probably from the extreme stress of the moment. Keith tried to calm her, but she insisted again. "Tell me what time it is! Hurry!"

Keith wanted to humor her, so he reached for the cell phone that he had removed and set aside before climbing in for the dirty task. "It's ten thirty. Why?"

"Is it really ten thirty-three?" Briana asked him again.

"Well, according to my phone, it's actually ten thirty-four, and it's set by satellite." He shot her another questioning look. "Do you need to be somewhere, or something?"

It was then that Briana showed him the silver pocket watch that had been buried with Mateo as his last request. The watch that needed to be carefully wound every night. She held it in her outstretched hands, like it was a baby bird she had found. It was open, and the face was clean due to its having been closed all this time. Keith looked at the time on the watch – ten thirty-three. He was about to marvel at the amazing coincidence of the watch having stopped at the very hour they had been there to exhume Mateo's bones, when Briana pointed to the second hand. It was still ticking!

Briana was thoroughly spooked, and couldn't go back in to finish the job, so Keith volunteered to take over from there. When they were finished, they signaled for the two groundskeepers to seal the crypt once again. Keith had to rearrange the bones in his box so that the lid would close, and they carried them to the family's niche where they would remain with the previously-deceased members of Mateo's ancestors.

Briana shook visibly as the two of them walked slowly to Mateo's home, where his sisters had planned a quiet meal in commemoration of the anniversary of their brother's passing. All along the way, she continued to watch the second hand tick away the minutes, in perfect time with the tourist's cell phone.

The meal was nice. Many of Mateo's favorite dishes had been prepared, and Alexandra had almost appeared to remember where she was a couple of times. Corina had made a colorful paper chain with the help of Lisbet and Heidi's grandchildren. Little Mateo was just learning to walk, and Heidi fussed over him. He couldn't keep his hands off of his great uncle's two-wheeled cart. There was noise and laughter and children of all ages, and Keith couldn't help but think it was just the way Mateo would have wanted. Still, he thought it was a real shame that he'd never learn the story behind the missing toe and the burn on his chest, or how it was that he had come to share a cigar with Che.

The following morning, Briana knocked on his door. He opened it to find her once again in tears, and once again with Mateo's pocket watch in her open hands.

This time, Keith could see just as clearly that the watch had stopped. It was nearly eleven by then, and Briana told him the watch had stopped at exactly six in the morning. She had tried to wind it, but it hadn't worked. She was going to bring it to the jeweler to see if he could fix it, and pass it down to little Mateo when he was older.

Keith stood motionless, staring off into space, as if looking for something hidden in the carpenter's house across the street. "Wait right here," he said to Briana. "Don't move."

He left her standing in the doorway for nearly five minutes before coming back with two tiny cups of coffee, and a bag that he had kept as a reminder of his friend. He clinked his cup to hers, and clinked the air above him, signaling to Mateo. Briana drank hers in the traditional two sip method, enjoying the taste of store-bought coffee that they didn't have the luxury of at her place. "That was a nice idea," she said to him.

"It wasn't mine, I'm afraid." He held his empty cup at arm's length, signaling to heaven. "Look closely at the time on the watch on the bag," he said, holding it to Briana. She had the watch in one hand and the bag in the other, both reading six a.m.

Coffee Time.

Brian Kerr has lived in Mexico for sixteen years with his Cuban wife and children, and works in the mining industry, which allows him hundreds of hours in airports and hotels, where he writes about his Cuban experiences.